Dear Rosemary —

If you picked up this
first edition for 50 ¢
hang on to it. It will be
worth a few bucks one
day. Best regards —

Yours, Harrison Cox.

Old Lyme
6/13/76

Books by **GEORGE HARMON COXE**

Murder with Pictures (1935)
The Barotique Mystery (1936)
The Camera Clue (1937)
Four Frightened Women (1939)
Murder for the Asking (1939)
The Glass Triangle (1939)
The Lady Is Afraid (1940)
No Time to Kill (1941)
Mrs. Murdock Takes a Case
    (1941)
Silent Are the Dead (1942)
Assignment in Guiana (1942)
The Charred Witness (1942)
Alias the Dead (1943)
Murder for Two (1943)
Murder in Havana (1943)
The Groom Lay Dead (1944)
The Jade Venus (1945)
Woman at Bay (1945)
Dangerous Legacy (1946)
The Fifth Key (1947)
Fashioned for Murder (1947)
Venturous Lady (1948)
The Hollow Needle (1948)
Lady Killer (1949)
Inland Passage (1949)
Eye Witness (1950)
The Frightened Fiancée (1950)
The Widow Had a Gun (1951)
The Man Who Died Twice
    (1951)
Never Bet Your Life (1952)
The Crimson Clue (1953)

Uninvited Guest (1953)
Focus on Murder (1954)
Death at the Isthmus (1954)
Top Assignment (1955)
Suddenly a Widow (1956)
Man on a Rope (1956)
Murder on Their Minds (1957)
One Minute Past Eight (1957)
The Impetuous Mistress (1958)
The Big Gamble (1958)
Slack Tide (1959)
Triple Exposure (1959), containing
    The Glass Triangle, The Jade
    Venus, and The Fifth Key
One Way Out (1960)
The Last Commandment (1960)
Error of Judgment (1961)
Moment of Violence (1961)
The Man Who Died Too Soon
    (1962)
Mission of Fear (1962)
The Hidden Key (1963)
One Hour to Kill (1963)
Deadly Image (1964)
With Intent to Kill (1965)
The Reluctant Heiress (1965)
The Ring of Truth (1966)
The Candid Impostor (1968)
An Easy Way to Go (1969)
Double Identity (1970)
Fenner (1971)
Woman with a Gun (1972)

These are Borzoi Books, published in New York by
ALFRED A. KNOPF

WOMAN
WITH
A GUN

WOMAN
WITH
A GUN

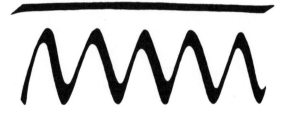

George Harmon Coxe

ALFRED A. KNOPF, New York

1972

THIS IS A BORZOI BOOK
PUBLISHED BY ALFRED A. KNOPF, INC.

Copyright © 1971 by George Harmon Coxe

All rights reserved under International and Pan-American Copyright
Conventions. Published in the United States by Alfred A. Knopf, Inc.,
New York, and simultaneously in Canada by Random House of Canada
Limited, Toronto. Distributed by Random House, Inc., New York.
Standard Book Number: 394–47441–4
Library of Congress Catalog Card Number: 75–171135

Manufactured in the United States of America

FIRST EDITION

For
MOTHER AGAIN

WOMAN
WITH
A GUN

1

SINCE WELL BEFORE DAWN the ketch *Annabel* had been heading north from St. George's, Grenada, keeping close in to the leeward shores of the Grenadines. Because of the prevailing winds she had been under power for the most part, and now, with little more than steerage-way, she was in the protected channel between the south coast of St. Vincent and Young's Island, her mooring a hundred yards or so from the Aquatic Club and dead ahead.

Fifty-two feet, beamy, and with comfortable freeboard, she would hardly have excited a modern-day yacht architect, for she had been native-built thirty-five years ago on the beach at Bequia, her fittings and the twenty-year-old diesel replacement imported from England. For all that, she made an excellent charter boat and was well suited to seas that were never smooth except close by a leeward shore.

At the moment Alan Maxwell was standing by the idling engine watching Oscar Jones, his mate, on the stubby bowsprit, a boathook in one hand, the other clamped about a stay as he leaned well out to snag the buoy.

He slipped the engine into neutral and kept his eye on the marker as he leaned outboard, one hand on the wheel.

Oscar, tall, straight, and muscular, remained poised like a spear-fisherman, gauging the angle of approach. Then, with a quick and expert dip of the hook he snagged the line and hauled back, bare feet braced now to take the way off.

"Okay?" Maxwell yelled, using only a touch of reverse as Oscar said, "Just fine, Mr. Max."

Glancing at the sky as he straightened and arched the small of his back, Maxwell saw that the threatening rain cloud was in a quadrant that would pass them by. At the same time a small, low-scudding patch cast its moving shadow over the ketch, and with it came an odd but disturbing premonition that made him wonder if the darkening of the sky at that moment could in some way be prophetic.

There was no reason for him to think so. But he was unable to forget other occasions when, after a period of complacency when life had seemed almost too wonderful, fate had lowered the boom and shattered such illusions with unforeseen reverses. For another fleeting moment he felt an unaccountable sense of dread that something would happen to spoil his long-awaited chance to re-establish himself in his profession and assure his future.

He was to recall this brief interlude of doubt later on. But now, with the cloud racing on and the sun bright again, he shook off the spell, telling himself that his bad luck was behind him. He'd had his tough break, and there remained only one tangible and easily explainable area for concern.

It was this particular problem that he'd been thinking about all the time he had been in Grenada having the shaft straightened and awaiting the air-express arrival of a new screw that had been ordered by cable from England.

Because of the unlucky necessity of these repairs, plus the cancellation of a week's charter on their account, he was five days overdue on his semi-annual mortgage payment of $1,500 plus interest at eight percent on the balance of $9,000 due on the *Annabel*. And although he had cabled the reasons for this technical default to George Osborne, the former owner, Osborne was an unpredictable man, and in recent months his attitude had been something less than friendly.

With only a gentle breeze stirring at the anchorage, and little tide, the mooring was quickly secured. The old-style gaff-rigged mainsail was already cradled, and Oscar busied himself with the staysail and jib. For Oscar needed no instructions. He probably knew more about handling the *Annabel* than Maxwell did because of his former service with Osborne; about his knowledge of the shores and reefs of the Grenadines and Tobago Cays there could be no doubt.

Native-born, he seldom used two words when one would do. A lithe, easy-moving man, age unknown but not old, he had a smooth brown skin and close-cropped hair that was tightly curled but not kinky. High cheekbones spoke of some Indian ancestor, possibly Carib, and this strain could have accounted for the reddish-brown pigmentation of his skin. Now, as Maxwell started below, he said:

"You'll be going ashore?"

"As soon as I change."

Maxwell had enjoyed the luxury of the main cabin, normally the province of the clients when on charter, for the past week. Forward were two double cabins, a head, and shower; beyond the bulkhead was the snug bow cabin with its angled bunks, head, and tiny basin that he shared with Oscar.

Stepping out of his soiled khaki shorts, he put on a clean white pair, a cotton jersey, denim slacks, socks, and loafers. When he had his dirty clothes bundled, he picked up a cord jacket that was somewhat rumpled but clean. Oscar was already in the dinghy which had been put over the side and taken in tow when they had Kingstown

abeam, but not until they were approaching the Aquatic
Club pier did he speak.

"The charter people come tomorrow?"

"The morning flight from Barbados."

"Two men and wives?"

"Well"—Maxwell grinned—"two men, anyway. I'm not
sure about the wife part. You remember Mr. Blake?"

"Oh yes, sir. From the time we spent those days on
Bastique. You wish to berth at Kingstown tomorrow for
provisions?"

"No. Tomorrow you stay home with your wife and kids.
I don't want to see you once you finish up this afternoon.
Tomorrow afternoon there'll be a big business deal be-
tween Mr. Blake and the Athertons at Hardin Hall—"

"About Bastique?"

"Right," Maxwell said, not surprised that Oscar had
guessed correctly.

"The Athertons, they sell the whole island?"

Maxwell said yes and changed the subject.

"My guess is that Blake won't want to start before Sunday morning. If they do some drinking Saturday night,
maybe not until Sunday afternoon. I'll know by tomorrow
night. Just be here early Saturday morning, okay?"

The Casurina Inn was the last in a row of beach houses
beyond the Aquatic Club, and the only two-story one.
Originally it had had a wide veranda on three sides. Now
only the front remained, the two sides having been built
out flush with the foundation to give more inside room.
Even so, there were only six upstairs rooms and a com-
munal bath at the rear end of the hall. Hardly more than
a guest house in spite of its name, its chief advantages to
Maxwell were that it was ideally located for his purpose,
and cheap.

Breakfast and dinner were served to those in residence,
but Maxwell paid a monthly rate for room only and signed

for whatever meals he took. Though there was no bar, you could generally find someone around at lunch and dinner time to make you a drink, and if you knew where to go, you could get ice.

The combination living-dining room was empty when Maxwell came through, but he went out back and found a maid to take his laundry. There were a few envelopes in his key slot behind the desk, and he skimmed through them as he went upstairs and down the hall. Three of them were bills from local merchants, and there were two cables, one from Blake confirming his arrival time and the other from Valerie Atherton asking him to meet the late-afternoon flight from Barbados.

Maxwell wasn't sure just when the idea came to him that his room had been searched during his absence. At first, there was nothing concrete about the impression, but as he admitted the possibility, he found confirmation in the distribution of his few possessions.

It was not, he knew, the work of the maid, who was allergic to most forms of labor. She made the bed when he was in residence, changed the sheets and left fresh towels once a week. But if he left things strewn around in the morning, they were usually in the same place when he returned. Even so, it was not until he opened the door of his one closet that he was sure. He had left the States with a B-4 bag, a suitcase, and a flight bag, and because of the way they were now stacked he knew someone had taken them out and put them back.

The two larger bags were empty, and the flight bag contained his passport, receipts, certain personal correspondence. He had no jewelry and he had long ago learned not to leave any cash around. This brought his attention to a tubular container of heavy cardboard similar to a fishing rod case. It was addressed to him and had been sent airmail, registered.

With more wonderment than concern working on him

and bringing a small frown to the corners of his eyes, he brought the tube to the table he used as a desk, removed the cap, and up-ended it to shake out several typewritten letters imprinted THE ISLAND DEVELOPMENT COMPANY and bearing a Boston address. By twisting his fingers inside he was able to withdraw some blueprints along with maps and overlays that were three feet wide and somewhat longer. Unrolling them, and anchoring the edges by the room's two ashtrays and a bottle of rum he kept locked away from the maid, he began to examine them in order.

The most recent letter read:

Dear Alan:

Enclosed is the plot plan for Bastique as we see it. The present owner's residence will be remodeled and used as you suggested during our last visit. The few native houses can remain by the landing jetty in the north cove and screened off from the rest of the development by a planting of some fast-growing trees or shrubbery.

The first nine holes of the golf course will be located as shown along with the second projected nine roughed out to give you an idea of the land involved. Your sketches and preliminary drawings of the Inn and six cottages meet with our approval and when we see you we can discuss the exact location of same.

As we have cautioned you before we believe that secrecy as to the details of our plan for the island is of great importance until payment has been made to the present owners and title is assured.

Albert Carswell has been given a hint that the island will be developed in the future but that is all. We prefer to keep it that way until we are ready to announce our overall plan.

Unless I cable you to the contrary we will arrive on the morning flight, Friday, February 12th.

Best regards,
Sam Blake

Putting the correspondence aside, Maxwell placed the government map of Bastique with it, and glanced at copies of blueprints of his own work. It was not until he examined the much larger map that had been made from the original, and studied the overlay which showed the size and location of all the lots and the paths to be cleared in place of roads, that he noticed anything wrong.

He nearly missed it because of the sense of pride and accomplishment that came to him each time he realized that he, Alan Maxwell, was to be the architect for the development—his first chance to practice his profession since coming here nearly two years earlier to buy the *Annabel* after his escape from Boston and a wife he could no longer tolerate.

Now, as he straightened and was about to remove his paperweights, his glance flicked past a pinhole in one corner of the map and overlay, snapped back, then narrowed in sharp focus.

The similar holes in the other three corners seemed so obvious that it was hard to understand how he had missed them. But they were there, in every sheet except the correspondence. Certain now that his hunch about the room had been right, he also knew why. Someone had thumbtacked those maps and sketches to the wall and photographed them; the inescapable conclusion followed that he was no longer the only one here who knew about the Island Development Company's plans for Bastique.

The very thought that the secret was out was instantly disturbing. He could not shake his concern as he began to collect the plans and correspondence, and once again he felt the thrust of that earlier and unwanted sense of foreboding that had seemed to warn of some impending, unforeseen trouble.

It took a conscious mental effort to dispel the mood, and when he had replaced the mailing tube he forced himself to marshal his thoughts, to make a mental list of those who might have wanted this information.

The list was short.

The Athertons, the present owners, would certainly be interested to know what would happen to the tiny island that had been in the family for generations. But he could not visualize the widow, Dorothy Atherton, going to such lengths. The same applied to Michael, who, as the older son, managed the St. Vincent plantations.

Even accepting the improbable, such new information would be academic. Why bother to photograph the details? The option to sell was binding so long as Island Development exercised it by Monday midnight and handed over their certified check for the balance due.

That left Albert Carswell.

Sam Blake's letter had stated that "a hint" had been given him. Had Carswell, for reasons of his own, decided he wanted more information? He already knew Maxwell was to be the architect for the proposed inn and cottages. He could further assume that Maxwell might well have information denied him. He would have had no problem searching the room since he had known Maxwell would be away most of the week—

The thought hung there as he moved to the rear window and stared sightlessly up the slope to the main highway that led to Calliaqua and on up the windward coast, his frown fixed, legs slightly spread, his body still.

He was a nicely proportioned man, with good shoulders, a muscular neck, and a face—well tanned but not burned— that was good-looking in an angular, bony way, though hardly handsome. The ears were a bit too prominent, the mouth too wide, a feature one forgot when he smiled, which was often. Certain vital statistics given in his expired Massachusetts driver's license stated that he would be thirty on his next birthday, that he had brown hair and eyes, that his height was five-ten and his weight 170.

As the seconds ticked by kitchen sounds came from the low attached structure at the rear. A donkey cart moved laboriously on the road, its driver hunched, the face obscured by the tattered wide-brimmed hat. The unexpected blast of the horn from an open-sided bus demanding that the cart make way shattered Maxwell's reverie; he blinked and forced his thoughts back to the moment.

"Old Albert?" he asked himself aloud. "Could be."

Thinking back about the man, he could admit he had never been entirely convinced that Carswell was altogether frank. As a local barrister with a none too busy practice, he was schooled in the longtime habit so characteristic of the legal profession, of admitting nothing that could be used against him or committing himself in any matter that might be viewed unfavorably.

Grunting softly, Maxwell swung away from the window. He had already formed a mental timetable for the remainder of the afternoon which listed three imperatives. The last, and best, would be meeting Valerie Atherton when she flew in from Barbados; but he could just as well pay a call on Carswell before having it out with George Osborne about the overdue payment on the *Annabel*.

2

ALBERT CARSWELL HAD HIS OFFICE and living quarters over an unprepossessing coral-and-wood building, the ground floor of which housed a pharmacy. There was a separate stairway tacked onto the right side, and jutting out from one corner at sidewalk level was a wrought-iron arm supporting a native-wood slab. Neatly burned into the weathered surface was a sign that read:

ALBERT CARSWELL
Barrister

—

Real Estate

The door at the upper landing stood open, and Alan Maxwell stepped into the entryway. On the right was a short hall which led to a comfortable living room, a bedroom, a small kitchen, and a bath, the bath itself consisting of an unfinished cement stall shower. The doorway on the left led directly to the front office, and Carswell was in his usual mid-afternoon place, a canvas planter's chair placed in front of the broad window overlooking the street and the harbor beyond.

He had yelled, "Come in!" when Maxwell knocked, and now, raising his shoulders and twisting his neck, he smiled and added, "Well, Alan. Come in, come in."

Levering himself out of the chair, he moved round a heavy native-built desk and sat down, waving his caller to the cane-bottom chair in front of him.

"Must have drifted off for a bit." He glanced at his watch, opened the center drawer of the desk, and removed a small plastic container. He tipped a pill into his palm and replaced the cap. When he had poured a little water from a battered carafe into a none too clean glass, he popped the pill into his mouth and swallowed, the up-and-down reflex of his Adam's apple distorting his scrawny throat. "Blood pressure," he said by way of explanation. "Something called aldactazide. Two a day."

Maxwell nodded and glanced about. It was a square, cool-looking room with bare board floors, an ancient couch, the desk, two other chairs similar to the one Maxwell took, and a bookcase filled with legal tomes that had somehow a dusty, unused look. Beyond the desk and over Carswell's head were two framed diplomas that Maxwell had never examined.

Now he leaned back and crossed his ankles, legs stretching as he reached for a cigarette. When he had a light he blew smoke at the barrister, and a slow grin touched his mouth.

"All set for tomorrow, Albert?"

"Oh, yes. Yes, indeed. I wasn't so sure about you. No trouble in Grenada?"

"None, once the propeller was flown in from England."

"I never did understand how you broke the original one in the first place."

"A water-logged palm bole we hit off the northeast coast of Bequia. We happened to have the engine working because that last party was in a hurry. Luckily the wind

was right to get us in and, more important, to take us to
Grenada more or less directly. Tell me, Albert," he added
in the same breath, "do you have a camera?"

Carswell showed surprise at the digression, blinked
once, tipped one long-fingered hand, and managed a smile
that held a suggestion of apology.

"An inexpensive Kodak Instamatic."

"That's all?"

"I find it sufficient for my needs."

"What needs?"

If Carswell took offense at Maxwell's persistence, it did
not show.

"As you know, I dabble in real estate from time to time.
I mean, quite aside from this Bastique thing. I find it helps
to have photographs of available properties to mail to
potential off-island renters or buyers."

Maxwell nodded as the other elaborated, but he was no
longer listening. Instead he let his thoughts drift back over
bits and pieces of information that had come to him from
time to time and which, when compiled, formed a sort of a
background for the man. The result was a mental image
that, though not necessarily accurate, was sufficient to
reach certain conclusions.

Physically, Albert Carswell was a thin, moderately tall
man with a somewhat hollow chest, a permanent stoop,
sparse, mousy hair and peanut-colored skin that sagged in
the long narrow face. His career as a barrister had been
undistinguished. Success in any form had somehow escaped
him; but he was accepted socially because of his family,
who at one time had owned a moderately prosperous
plantation. For all that, it was through his efforts and his
alone that the Bastique project had been born.

Occasionally ebullient in manner, his washed-out blue
eyes more often had a look of patient suffering. His daytime dress was invariably a white drill suit, yellowed some
from the sun and frequent washings and, more often than

not, complete with vest. He had a pedantic, courtly way of speaking, possibly cultivated to give strangers the impression of a superior background and a prominent place in the social and business life of the community.

Actually, he had for years managed no more than a hand-to-mouth existence. As a barrister, his practice was uncertain and seldom very profitable. Occasional commissions on real estate deals and rentals allowed him to have a part-time maid who came mornings to get his breakfast, make his bed, and do a bit of dusting.

By eleven-thirty every morning he could be found at the City Club for a game of dominoes and three rum cocktails, made in the old-fashioned way with a pitcher and a swizzle stick, and knocked back while the bead was still on the drink. Following this ritual would come a meager lunch consisting of the soup of the day and a piece of fish or a sandwich. Afternoons would find him just where Maxwell had—in the chair for a nap, unless interrupted by an unexpected client.

If his father had concentrated on the family estate, there might have been something for Carswell to inherit. But unfortunate trades on the Canadian and London stock exchanges had dissipated the assets, so that when the old man died in his sleep the plantation had to be sold to take care of the mortgages and taxes. Fortunately Albert had his law degree from McGill by that time and had married a girl from Barbados. Maxwell wasn't sure how long it had lasted; he did know that the wife had left Carswell a dozen or so years before, taking a small daughter with her. No one seemed to know if he ever heard from her, or even if he cared. The history of two brothers who had fled the island after the estate was settled was equally vague.

But Carswell was persistent in his belief that one day the Fates would smile on him. To hurry that day along, he concentrated on the sale of Bastique. The one building of any importance there was called The Residence and was used by the family from time to time on holidays and occasionally offered for rent. In addition, there were a few small houses for the native families, including the caretaker. Abortive attempts had been made long ago to raise a paying crop, and cattle had similarly been tried without much success. The families were allowed a small plot to raise vegetables; some had a cow or a couple of pigs or a goat, and all raised chickens. A certain amount of fishing augmented the diet.

But there was no electric power, no telephone, no communication with the outside world except by small boat. In spite of these drawbacks, Carswell never lowered his sights. Whenever he had a bit of cash to spare, he would advertise in the London *Times* or *Town and Country*, or take an inch or so in the edition of the *Wall Street Journal* that featured such offerings . . .

"I'm sorry, Albert," Maxwell said, aware somehow that the man was waiting for a reply to some unheard question. He leaned forward to grind out his cigarette stub. "I was daydreaming."

Carswell accepted the apology with a wave of his hand and a small smile: "About the continuing and profitable advancement of our mutual endeavors, I hope."

"Something like that." Maxwell grinned back at him. "I've got to hand it to you, Albert," he said, and meant it.

"Hand it to me?"

"You never gave up, did you? All those ads—"

Carswell seemed pleased at the implied compliment but answered modestly: "They say you have to believe, Alan. I was convinced that some day one small advertisement would appear in the right publication at the right time to be seen by the right man. All I had to do was bring the parties together and then convince Dorothy Atherton that the price was right.

"As a matter of fact, I think Island Development is making a very sound investment. Don't you? Of course," he added, not waiting for a reply, "the new airstrip here was a factor, but not the only one. All these Island Development people had to do is to look what's happening elsewhere. Those American national chains like Hilton and Holiday building new accommodations in Tobago and Grenada. Bastique, because of the character of the land, could be equally successful.

"Why, once your inn is up and the travel agencies are aware of the advantages," he added, warming to his subject, "what's to prevent the new owners from laying out building sites along the shores of the lagoon? Perhaps even a golf course. The land is ideal. Rolling. No hills. No woods to be cleared except near the north shore, which I imagine will be left as it is. Don't you agree?"

For another moment, the small mental burr of suspicion that had arisen in his room demanded attention, and Maxwell said:

"Have you any reason to believe they plan such an expansion?"

"None. That is, nothing definite. Still, you must admit such a possibility. The unique geography of the island favors such a move, wouldn't you say?"

"In what way?"

"The lagoon, for instance. Because of its very nature it offers developers twice the number of waterfront plots that would be available on an ordinary coastline."

And Maxwell was forced to admit that Carswell was right. Whatever the accident of nature that had forced the earth's upheaval and created the Windward and Leeward islands, it had left Bastique one of the very few without the characteristic rugged contours. From St. Kitts south to Trinidad the islands Maxwell had seen were mountainous in varying degrees. Some, like Dominica and Martinique and Guadeloupe, had peaks that were often cloud-shrouded; the same was true of St. Vincent, particularly the extinct volcano La Soufrière. Only Barbados, which was more coral than volcanic, and to a lesser degree Antigua, could boast of much more than hills of perhaps a thousand or twelve hundred feet.

Bastique was like that, a sort of Barbados in miniature. With its highest point hardly more than four hundred feet above sea level, it was gently rolling toward the south and shaped like a lobster claw. The broad end, more rugged and somewhat wooded, pointed almost due north, with only the covelike little harbor protected. The opened pincers pointing to the south formed the palm-studded, sandy lagoon that cut perhaps a quarter of the way into the mile-and-a-half-long island, its channel deep enough to accommodate nearly any pleasure boat not depending entirely on sails . . .

He snapped his mind back again, and asked, "How many prospective customers have you had for Bastique since you've been trying to sell it? How many bites?"

"Too many. It all came down to a matter of price. Thirty years ago you could have bought the island for one hundred and fifty thousand American. Unfortunately as the cost of living went up, so did the price. As I said, the airstrip here was a tremendous help, and then, of course, what created the recent interest was all the publicity and pictures of that French liner *Antilles* that went aground on the reef not far from Bastique. . . . What a waste. Can you explain what that fool captain was doing there? His last port of call was Caracas, or rather La Guaira, wasn't it? How would you have come?"

"Straight up, keeping well off the Grenadines until he had Bequia on the starboard quarter. An eighty degree turn to starboard, and plenty of water all the way to Barbados."

"He said the charts were wrong."

"Could be."

"But what do you think put him there?"

"As a guess, I'd say he wanted to save a little time. Somewhere south of Bequia he turned northeast to cut between Bequia and Bastique. He could have made it, but with twenty thousand tons under him it had to be risky."

He stopped, glanced at his strapwatch, and realized he was wasting time in chatter. He thought again about the thumbtack holes and then tried not to. He grinned at Carswell and stood up.

"One lousy little ad in the *Wall Street Journal* turned the trick, didn't it, Albert? Now you'll have your bonanza, and I must say you earned it."

"Bonanza?"

"Five percent of $370,000 is a nice piece of change."

Carswell preened a bit, ran his palms over his wide lapels, and pulled to attention a tie that was noticeably frayed at the knot.

"And only the beginning, I hope, Alan," he said. "By that I mean, if my speculation as to further development is valid, I might manage to be appointed the local representative for Island Development. To handle inquiries, perhaps earn a commission or two in case the company decides to sell lots from time to time.

"As a matter of fact"—he stood up, lights dancing in his eyes and his dentures showing—"I've been meaning to ask if you could see your way clear to putting in a good word for me, should the occasion arise. After all, you will be working rather closely with Mr. Blake."

Maxwell nodded and slung the cord jacket over his shoulder. He said he would be glad to.

3

GEORGE OSBORNE OWNED a modest two-bedroom house partway up the hill in back of downtown Kingstown. He had shared this with his daughter since the death of his wife some years earlier, except for the two years the girl had been at school in Canada.

The yard was small and fenced in, as was the custom in the neighborhood, not only to give some semblance of privacy but to discourage light-fingered islanders who were not against a bit of breaking and entering but disliked a frontal approach. Maxwell parked his secondhand Consul as far off the side of the road as he could, walked through the open gate and up the drive.

The only porch of any consequence was at the rear of the house, and overlooked the Playing Field where Osborne could follow the Sunday cricket matches with his binoculars as well as observe the activity in the harbor and roadstead. Vines, mostly bougainvillea, choked the fence, and there was a tall spreading breadfruit tree and the bareish, odd-looking conformation of a frangipani not yet in bloom.

Osborne was on the porch, as Maxwell knew he would be at this time of day, when his daughter was due back from her job as secretary to the local bank manager. He too was in a canvas chair, though not one with the nearly horizontal back of the planter variety.

He interrupted his harbor-scanning sufficiently to turn his head, and his welcome was a noncommittal grunt. He waited until his caller had, without invitation, selected a wicker chair, and his opening remark was characteristic:

"So you got back, hunh?"

Since no reply was expected. Maxwell made none. There would, he knew, be other uncomplimentary remarks until Osborne got whatever he was brooding about out of his system.

It had not always been like that. Osborne had been friendly and obliging when Maxwell and his new wife Louise had spent a week of their honeymoon aboard the *Annabel.* The friendliness along with an air of goodwill had persisted when Maxwell had fled Boston and made him an offer for the ketch. They had dickered some over price, but there had been no serious disagreement over the down payment and the terms of the existing mortgage. The change had come more recently, and Maxwell attributed it to two factors that were in no way connected.

Perhaps the more important of these was the man's physical condition. Strong-looking and a good six feet tall, he had a lot of graying hair, steady gray eyes, and a weathered, square-cut face. But he'd had two heart attacks, the second one severe and leading to the medical ultimatum that decreed he give up his boat and take it easy. It was his hands, however, that gave him the most trouble. Corded and still powerful when he had something substantial to grip, the fingers were gnarled, bent, painful, and lacking in mobility, a condition that could never improve.

His blunt, no-nonsense manner had given way to a habitual grouchiness that only his daughter could control. Her name was Wanda and she was twenty-four, and Osborne's one remaining aim in life was to see that she married Michael Atherton and became mistress apparent to Hardin Hall and the family plantation. In this he had the full cooperation of Michael's mother, Dorothy.

The fact that there had not yet been a formal announcement of the engagement apparently was Michael's fault. That the marriage would take place was understood but seldom mentioned, except when Osborne and Dorothy got together at the Hall for their weekly round of cribbage. Michael, it seemed, would not be hurried. Subservient in most things to his strong-willed mother, this was an area where he refused to listen; for her part, Wanda Osborne was too shy to take the initiative.

She was also, however, too independent to sit and wait for Michael's too-infrequent calls; and that is how Maxwell had got into the picture. With little local talent available either for him or for her, they had somehow established a friendly but purely platonic relationship which resulted in dinner together once or twice a month, an occasional stop at the local movie house, an early return.

At first, Osborne had accepted the arrangement with a kind of good-natured reluctance. This, however, had finally given way to downright disapproval. Hints to his daughter had done no good, and he took the direct approach to Maxwell by stating he would appreciate it if the custom was discontinued, implying that nothing should be done that would in any way court Michael Atherton's disapproval. Such bluntness brought a reply in kind which pointed out that Wanda was a woman, and of age, and as such the decision should be hers . . .

"What?" he said, aware that Osborne had spoken.

"I said, if you'd been under sail like you should have been you'd never have bent the shaft or ruined the screw."

It took a second more for Maxwell to tune in the remark. He knew the matter of the overdue mortgage payment would be brought up soon enough. He had an idea the discussion might be unpleasant. He wanted it over with, but decided it would be unwise to show his impatience.

"Anyone could hit a water-logged palm bole," Osborne continued, "but from where you were you didn't need the damn engine to bring her in."

"The clients were in a hurry. With the engine—"

"I know." Osborne's grunt was uncomplimentary. "So that added two, maybe three knots. You'd save—"

"I know what I'd save," Maxwell said, his mood beginning to match Osborne's and his dark eyes resentful. "I told you the party wanted to get back in time to—"

"What'd it cost you for your piece of foolishness?"

"What difference does it make?"

"Maybe quite a bit. Your payment is five days overdue."

"Because I had to cancel last week's charter. I'm booked for the coming week. A thousand U.S. net. If I can get a big advance tomorrow, and I think I can—"

"According to the terms of our agreement you have already defaulted," Osborne said coldly, ignoring the explanation. "All I'd have to do is get a court order tomorrow and you know what would happen?"

He leaned sideways and tapped Maxwell's knee. "The *Annabel* would be impounded, or whatever they call it. You'd be locked out. At the proper time she'd be put up at public auction. If the sale brought more than ninety-three hundred and sixty dollars the difference would be yours . . . By the way," he added, a note of malice in his tone, "there's a lady been in town the past week asking for you."

"A lady?" Maxwell thought fast, swallowed, his eyes instantly concerned as some unaccountable sense of apprehension and foreboding slithered through his brain. "Who?"

"Your wife. Name's Louise, isn't it?"

For a long, startled moment Maxwell could only stare at Osborne, eyes widening with shock and disbelief as he searched desperately for some hint that this was somehow part of a bad joke.

He said, "You're kidding," his voice rasping and his throat dry. The steady gray gaze gave him no hope. Even so, feeling as though someone had slugged him under the heart, and with the bottom dropping slowly out of his stomach, he tried again: "Here?"

"Staying at the Villa Inn."

Maxwell understood finally that what he was hearing must be the truth but traces of shock and dismay still lingered and he had trouble with his words.

"How—how long has she been here?"

"Five—six days."

"You've met her?"

"I have."

"Where?"

"She came to see me."

"Why?"

"She said she had some business to discuss . . . I remembered her from the time you chartered the *Annabel* for your honeymoon," Osborne continued—this last mostly to himself. He took a breath, and now there was a vicious, almost hateful edge to his tone that Maxwell had never heard before; neither could he understand it.

"The way she used to rub up against you every chance she got. Half naked all of the time, with no clothes at all when she sunned herself up by the bow and then diving in like that when we were anchored and whenever it pleased her and never caring who saw her."

His mouth twisted as though he were about to spit. "Like a common tart," he said, "as if the fact that she was filthy rich changed anything. It was beyond me even in those first days how or why you married her unless it was for her money. Oh, she was attractive enough, and you could tell she knew how to use that sexy body of hers. You seemed a pretty decent, level-headed young man, but you know, before you left, all I felt for you was pity."

He leaned back, gray eyes focused now and probing:

"You lasted nine months, is that what you told me when you came here? She chased you out?"

"I ran," Maxwell said, and knew it was the literal truth. "How did she know I was here?" he asked half aloud and not really caring.

"If you want my opinion—" Osborne stopped, considered, began again. "You recall the man who calls himself Leon Carr, who came to the island about three weeks ago?"

"That tall blond guy staying at the Pelican? Supposed to be looking for property to build a new hotel?"

"That was his story, and he went through the motions, questioning everyone who'd listen, hiring a car and traipsing about with his cameras."

"What about him?"

"I think he is what you would call a phony, a private investigator, who tracked you here and compiled a little dossier on you and your affairs to turn over to that miserable little bitch—"

He stopped again, choking on his anger, and it was now so obvious that Maxwell put aside his own troubled thoughts to ask about it.

"What's bugging you?" he asked flatly. "Why should you give a damn what—"

The sound of a car stopping on the road out front made him hold the question, and as he turned he saw Wanda Osborne step down and walk up the drive. As she came up on the porch and smiled at them, he realized that the inner shaking that had started with Osborne's announcement was under control; so were his thoughts.

"Hello, Father . . . and Alan," she said, sounding very pleased as he stood up. She stooped to kiss her father's cheek and then, noting the empty table in front of them, eyed him severely. "You haven't even offered him a drink?"

"I've had no time," Osborne said in a soft growl that was full of pride and affection. "We've been discussing business."

"That's no excuse," she said in mock rebuke. "What can I get you, Alan?"

"His favorite is sugarcane brandy, but we have none," Osborne said.

"A whisky-soda would be fine," Maxwell said.

They both watched her disappear into the inner shadows of the house, and there was approval in Maxwell's glance as a descriptive word came to him. It was not a word you could ever tell a girl. *Beautiful, lovely, glamorous, sexy*— those were the acceptable adjectives. The word he had in mind was trite but, in its best sense, it had to be a compliment.

The word was *nice*; and this was one of the nicest girls he had ever known. She had a nicely rounded figure that might someday be plump; she had a nice disposition, a nice manner, a nice smile. About five foot six, he thought, with medium blond hair worn straight and shoulder length, a lovely complexion, and a rather plain and unassuming prettiness. The large hazel eyes had some shyness in them but were striking when she looked right at you. She was a girl that people smiled at, women as well as men, because they knew her smile was altogether genuine.

He was still watching the doorway and thinking fondly of her when she came back with a tray. She put his whisky-soda in front of him, put a smaller glass in front of her father—Maxwell knew it was a pink gin with ice—and began to open three small containers containing medication. She shook out three pills and a blue-and-white capsule.

"You'll take these first," she said.

"All right, all right." Osborne accepted them. "A damned old crock," he grumbled, and shook a pill in his palm. "Digitoxin for my tricky heart. Indocin"—he added the blue-and-white capsule—"for confounded crippled aching hands; supposed to keep down the inflammation of my joints. Four times daily. These I eat," he said about the two remaining tablets. "You can guess what they are."

"Aspirin?"

"Correct." He arranged the medication in his palm, popped the four into his mouth, and washed them down with a swallow of pink gin.

The girl re-capped the bottles. "He knows they do him good and he suffers without them," she said. "And still he grumbles . . . Were you serious about talking business?"

Osborne sighed, shrugged. "I'm afraid so, my dear, but it shouldn't take long now."

He leaned back when she had left, sipped his gin, and looked out over the harbor, distance in his gaze. When he made no immediate effort to resume their discussion, Maxwell began to recall the bits of information he had picked up here and there during his island stay.

Unlike Albert Carswell, Osborne was British-born, and had had his primary education in England. He had never gone beyond the equivalent of an American high school and had come here with his father and mother when the father was sent out to take over a shipping agency representing several lines. This was in the days before there was any air service, when the inter-island schooners had greater importance, when passenger ships made regular calls, chiefly a Canadian line scheduled between Halifax and British Guiana.

Before the father's death he had acquired four native-built schooners, and this was what George Osborne had inherited. The sudden, tragic and unexpected death of his wife from a brain hemorrhage when his daughter was small had, to all accounts, changed the man greatly. Unable to shake off his loss, he had begun to take increasingly to the bottle. Wanda had been sent to Barbados for additional schooling, and the sale of two schooners had given her two more years in Canada.

The *Annabel*, which had been finished shortly before Osborne's father's death, had served a variety of purposes. Built originally for pleasure and used with friends for a day or a weekend, it had been leased from time to time for charter work. But Osborne had not taken personal charge until he had disposed of the remaining two schooners and put the proceeds into a modest annuity. This, and what he was getting for the ketch, plus the house, were all that was left.

Now aware, finally, of his thoughts and the continuing silence, Maxwell glanced at Osborne. Still motionless, his gaze seaward, the weathered face had settled into hard grim lines, the brows warped with brooding. Maxwell put his glass down and cleared his throat to get attention.

"You were about to tell me how you developed such a hate for my wife."

Osborne swiveled his head, blinked twice. It seemed to take him a second or two to realize where he was and who had asked the question.

"It's what she's done to Michael Atherton," he said bitterly. "I can't understand the lad; it is beyond my comprehension. In five days' time she has him wrapped round her little finger and eating out of her hand. Twice now they've had dinner at the Villa Inn. Once he came home at one in the morning; the last time it was after three. He has always listened to his mother, but not now. She's told me of their bitter quarrel, Michael as stubborn as a mule and threatening to leave the Hall."

He turned, things happening behind the gray eyes so that Maxwell could not tell if what he saw was disgust, dismay, or the reflection of some inner fear.

"Tell me," Osborne said. "How could a woman turn a man's head like that? Thirty years old and always with his feet on the ground, courting my daughter like the gentleman he is—"

"She did it to me," Maxwell said. "And two others before me."

"In five days?"

"It could have happened in five days if *I'd* had the time
to spend with her. And I was my own man, with no mother
to please or be concerned about. A guy like Michael,
brought up as he was, would be a pushover."

"But why, man?" There was a touch of anguish in the
tone now. "Tell me."

"How do I know?" Maxwell said, his annoyance showing,
but directed more at himself and his memories than at
Osborne. "She's smart, intelligent, wealthy; she's spent
years developing the necessary tricks to get her own way.
She has style, a pretty face, and a lovely body. She knows
all there is to know about sex and she's just aggressive
enough to let you know she wants it and at the same time
make you think her advances are refined and virginal, even
though you know better."

He swore softly, and was surprised to hear the vehemence of his tone.

"She's got everything it takes," he said irritably. "Didn't
you ever hear of flattery? She'll flatter you out of your skull
and make you like it. She does the courting, damn it. How
is a nice country boy like Michael, who may live like a
monk for all I know, going to stand up against a woman
like that? Five days with her when *you* were thirty and
you'd be begging for it."

He stopped abruptly, aware that his question was rhetorical, and determined to say no more. When he looked
at Osborne, he was astonished to see the lines of weariness
and defeat around the mouth and eyes. He had slumped in
his chair, his crippled fingers clasping his empty glass. Not
knowing what else to say, Maxwell started to get up; then
he remembered why he had come. He reached out and
touched Osborne gently on the arm.

"About that mortgage, George."

"What?" Osborne was having trouble concentrating.

"The mortgage. I know I'm late, but you know why.
Those things happen. I mean about the shaft and prop.
I can give you a thousand in the morning—"

Something about Osborne's expression checked him and
he stopped. A flush had tinged the weathered cheeks and
the gray eyes seemed evasive and embarrassed. Suspicious
and conscious of some new uncertainty, he said:

"What's the matter?"

Osborne studied his hands and shifted uncomfortably in
his chair.

"You can give me a week for the balance, can't you?"
Maxwell pressed, not understanding the other's silence.

"It isn't that, Alan."

"It isn't what?"

"It's too late for a payment, any payment. I mean to me."

Maxwell took a slow deliberate breath and tried to control his impatience.

"How is it too late?"

"Because the mortgage isn't mine. Not anymore. I sold
it, signed it over."

"You did *what*? Signed it to who?"

"Your wife. She paid me off in full. She has the papers,
everything."

Maxwell heard the words clearly. He understood each
and every one, and yet his reaction took a little time. He
sat tense and immobile, a strange fluttering in the emptiness of his stomach. His speechlessness gave way to a slow
bewilderment, and then came the hot and flaring anger.
Osborne took the brunt of it even as instinct and intuition
had begun to warn Maxwell that he had lost the *Annabel*.

"You bastard!" he said, his voice thin, controlled, and
vicious. "You miserable bastard! You know what will happen, don't you? You tell me you hate my wife's guts and
yet you sell me out."

He swore again, very softly. When he could speak
evenly, his voice was flat and contemptuous.

"Okay, George. I knew you didn't like me much. You've been giving me the shaft ever since I started taking Wanda out once in a while. She could have told you—and probably did—that it didn't mean a thing. But I never thought you disliked me enough—"

"That's not it!" Osborne said, interrupting. "I didn't like the idea of you taking Wanda around, no. But that's not the point."

"No? Then what *is* the point?"

"You've got to understand."

Osborne's obvious earnestness and distress demanded attention; Maxwell looked directly at him, dark gaze bleak and challenging.

"Okay, George," he said again. "Make me understand. Give it a try, anyway."

Osborne became aware of the way his crippled fingers were clamped about his empty glass. He put it down, still hesitating, as though trying to compose his thoughts. When he spoke, it was in the tone and manner of a supplicant.

"She came to me early in the week and spoke about the boat and your debt."

"How would she know about it so quick?"

"I didn't wonder about it then. Now I think it was that Carr fellow. Hell, Alan, this is a small place. Everyone in the club knew·about you and me and the boat and the mortgage and how you've been working to pay it off. You've become a very popular lad here, and if I tried to shut you out for being a week late, my friends would have run me out of town . . . All Carr had to do was keep asking questions. You see that, don't you?"

"So she came to you and put on an act."

"Exactly. I remembered her, of course. I knew you'd left her, but I had no idea why. She spoke of that. She said the whole thing had been her fault and she finally realized it. She wanted to surprise you, and if she could buy my interest it would make a fine peace offering. She wanted to make you a present." He tipped one hand in a gesture of resignation.

"I knew she was a wealthy woman. She made it sound right and reasonable. You spoke of flattery. Well, I suppose I fell for it too. I'm sorry. She was so damn sweet and persuasive I didn't think to doubt her."

"Yeah," Maxwell said, understanding full well how such a thing could happen. He could almost see and hear Louise putting on her act.

"What do you think will happen?" Osborne asked anxiously.

"I think she'll show up when she's ready with a police constable and the proper papers and throw me off."

"Maybe not."

"How do you figure?"

"She gave me the check Sunday. I didn't go downtown Monday, so I didn't deposit it. On Tuesday Dorothy Atherton told me how your wife was working on Michael, and I got an idea of the kind of person she really was. I still have the check. I can say I won't go through with it."

"And what will the courts say if she fights it?"

"Who can say? The point is, we can delay it, wear her down. After that—"

He stopped, his glance shifting beyond, and when Maxwell turned he saw Wanda in the shadow of the doorway. She wore a light robe, her cheeks were shiny and fresh-looking, and she had a towel wrapped turbanlike about her head.

"I washed my hair," she said. "Time out from business," she added, and looked at her father. "How long has Alan been sitting there with an empty glass? Did I hear someone yelling?"

"Me, I guess," Maxwell said, already on his feet. "Sometimes when I get real interested in an argument I have a tendency to shout . . . No thanks, Wanda," he said when she reached for his glass. He glanced at his watch. "I have to meet the Barbados plane."

"Valerie?"

"Yes."

"I heard she was coming this weekend."

Maxwell glanced at Osborne, who made a small shrugging gesture and said he was glad Maxwell had stopped in and was sure things would work out. Maxwell said he'd see Wanda at the Hall sometime this weekend and she said she hoped so.

4

THE ARNOS VALE AIRSTRIP was little more than two miles
from Kingstown, and Valerie Atherton's flight was a pinpoint in the eastern sky when Alan Maxwell parked and
walked toward the small terminal building where he
watched the aircraft pass to one side, losing height as it
banked for its approach into the wind.

The morning flight was a Viscount that came down from
Antigua by way of St. Lucia and Barbados, continuing on
to Grenada and Trinidad, from which it returned late in
the day. This one, a Twin Beech with a shorter range,
made the triangle of Barbados–St. Vincent–Grenada–
Barbados.

He was waiting in the doorway when Valerie, who had
been making the weekend trip every two or three weeks
for some time, was waved through customs—a formality
for her, because she had plenty of clothes at Hardin Hall
and seldom carried more than an overnight case and a
flight bag.

The sight of her smile and the slender supple body that
always moved with grace made things stir pleasantly inside
him. For she was a vital, spirited girl with a mind of her

own and a smooth flawless skin, slightly tanned and need-
ing little make-up. The well-spaced green eyes gave an
impression of warmth and intelligence, so that it was at
once a face worth looking at. Her dark brown hair showed
auburn glints when the light was right, and her feather cut
usually had a slightly windblown look, making it difficult
at times to resist running his fingers lightly through it to
feel its fine texture.

She was wearing a tailored navy suit of some lightweight
material that looked like linen, and the skirt, not quite a
mini, was short enough to show the beginnings of well-
shaped thighs and tell you the rest was very nice indeed.
Now, as he took her bags, she leaned to kiss him on the
cheek and clamped one arm inside his elbow.

"You got my cable? Good. I wasn't sure you'd be in."

"This afternoon."

The sense of pleasure that had come with their meeting
did not last long since it could not survive the smoldering
thought of his wife actually being on the island, let alone
what she had done to him. He drove moderately, eyes
fixed on the coast road and its traffic mixture of cars, buses,
trucks, donkey carts, and bicycles. He had gone perhaps
three miles when he felt the hand on his arm and turned
to find the green eyes appraising him.

"What is it, Alan?"

"What?" He knew he sounded stupid.

"You've been brooding about something ever since we
started."

"I have?"

"Really glowering, you know?"

"I'm sorry." He grinned at her, but she sensed it was an
effort. After a few seconds while he searched for something
to say, she added:

"Bad news? Would you want to talk about it?"

"It might help. But not here. I can't drive and talk. I'm

too burned up. Can you put up with me for another five minutes . . . It's my wife," he said, aware that there was no longer any point in keeping silent.

"Oh." The voice was curiously soft. "Has something happened?"

"She's on the island. Has been nearly a week. And raising hell as usual."

The blank statement silenced her, for she was too intelligent and considerate to pry. This gave him time to think back over their relationship the past year or so.

During this time he had learned quite a lot about her and had acquired a sketchy history of the last two generations of Athertons. The family had been planters on the island for well over a hundred years—he was not sure when the first Atherton arrived or how they acquired Bastique—and apparently had always been people of substance.

Valerie's father had been born here, the younger son. He had been educated in Canada and, after a brief fling at helping run the family holdings, had gone back there to make a business career. When the war came he had managed a desk commission, and for a time had been stationed in Philadelphia on some sort of procurement job. It was there that he met and married Valerie's mother, who had been born in one of the suburbs. After the war he had returned to Canada to resume his business career, remaining there until the death of his brother—the father had died shortly before that—forced him to return and take over the family estates.

There had been three children, and Michael, being the oldest and therefore expected to take over the business, had been sent to the agricultural college in Port of Spain. Ian, next in line, more spirited and independent, had managed to get away for college and medical school in London, where he now practiced.

Valerie, equally spirited and arguing that she was half American, knowing also how to handle her father, had gone to finishing school in New England and then to one of the country's top secretarial schools in Boston. She had been working for an insurance company when her father died, returning to the island like a dutiful daughter when her mother insisted. But not for long.

St. Vincent bored her, and when she threatened rebellion a compromise was reached which enabled her to get a job in the Barbados office of British West Indies Airlines. More recently, she had shifted to the local radio-TV outfit called Rediffusion, and now had a twice-weekly half-hour morning talk show.

They were past the first hills now, and a sloping, plateau-like area stretched ahead for a mile or so. All of it from the bluff overlooking the sea to the mountain ridge rising on the left was under cultivation. The drive to Hardin Hall was coming up now, and when he had made the gradual right turn, he put the gearshift in neutral, cut the motor, and pulled to a stop on a grassy strip just off the coral drive.

He sighed audibly as he collected his thoughts and brought out cigarettes, wondering whether or not he should tell this girl some of the things he had heretofore been careful to avoid. For in the time he had known her, there had never been any talk of love or marriage between them. She had been told early that he was married and had left his wife. He knew that she had a boyfriend of sorts in Barbados, a young Englishman who had tried other things and was at present managing a small hotel on the St. Lawrence coast.

He did not know how intimate or serious this relationship was, nor did he care; at least that is what he always told himself. It was enough that Valerie liked him and seemed to enjoy his company to the point, he liked to think, that she looked forward to seeing him on weekend visits such as these. The relationship had continued warm, friendly, and semi-platonic.

At no time, though the idea had suggested itself on occasion, had there been tentative gropings for breast or thigh on the front seat of the car. A warm and affectionate kiss, not too lingering and not too frequent, was sufficient to express how they felt and seemed to indicate a mutual understanding and a complete lack of embarrassment. Now, when she had her light, she expelled the first puff and twisted on the seat to face him, her smile softly quizzical.

"Have you seen her?" she asked, as there had been no interruption and the continuity of thought was understood.

"No."

"How did you find out?"

"From George Osborne. Just a little while ago. She's been at the Villa Inn for the past six days according to him. You didn't know about her?"

"Of course not." She tipped her chin, eyes narrowing. "How could I?"

"I thought you might have heard from your mother this week. Osborne tells me she's pretty upset—so is he."

"About what, for heaven's sake?"

"It seems Louise, my good and persistent wife, has been making meaningful passes at your brother."

"Michael?" Her laugh was quick, genuine, and just slightly tinged with doubt. "But that's absurd. In six days? Please, Alan, not Michael."

"Would you believe he was out with her, at least he didn't come home, until one o'clock in the morning and three a.m. another time?"

The quiet seriousness of this statement sobered her, and her concern showed in the sharper cadence of her voice.

"Just what is it she wants? Why is she here? Did George tell you that?"

"I'm going to find out as soon as I take you home. I imagine her primary purpose is to make things just as tough for me as she can."

"After all this time? And how would she know you were here?"

Maxwell spoke of the man he knew as Leon Carr and Osborne's conclusion that Carr was a private investigator hired by his wife not only to locate him but to find out everything he could about what had been happening. Then, not giving her a chance to interrupt, he went on quickly, his tone clipped and resentful as he spoke of the basic facts he had been told by Osborne.

When he finished she leaned forward to put her cigarette out in the dashboard ashtray, her gaze troubled and a frown marring the smoothness of her brow.

"You think she intends to take the *Annabel*?"

"As a guess, yes. But only after she tries to make me crawl a bit."

She nodded, no longer looking at him. "Perhaps," she said, "you'd better tell me about her and your marriage and just why you came here in the first place. You never have, you know."

"It'll take a while."

"I have time if you have."

Somehow the invitation was a welcome one, and for the first time he found he was eager to express feelings too long bottled up, to cleanse himself, to see if he could make this girl understand.

"The only thing I knew about her in the beginning was that she was wealthy and had made the society pages from time to time. She knew the senior partner of the firm I worked for socially, and because of her connections had been able to throw some business our way. She was just a name to me until she wanted some additions made to a house she had on Cape Cod and I was elected to take charge. It didn't take her too long to convince me she was in love with me. Don't ask me why. I don't know now and I didn't then. I doubt if I could make you understand."

"Try."

"She told me she had been married twice, but the reasons she gave for the breakups had little basis in truth—as I found out later. I suppose I was just too gullible. Like most guys, I expected to get married some day and here was a pretty girl with a lovely body, a convincing manner which made her both appealing and lovable, and a feline cunning which was impossible to resist for a simple-minded character like me. I was impressed, flattered, receptive to any and all demands and hardly able to accept my good fortune. To put it bluntly, she conned me and I was an eager and willing victim."

"Conned?" He glanced round to find her looking at him. "I may know what that means, but tell me anyway."

The suggestion of humor in her remark helped make things easier, and he found he could manage a grin.

"I guess it comes from 'confidence man.' Roughly, it means someone who sells you something you don't want but makes you think you do until after you've bought it."

"I understand."

"For instance, *she* set the wedding date. *She* bought her own engagement ring. I wanted to buy a two-carat diamond which would set me back two thousand bucks, a sizable outlay for a guy like me. *She* wanted an emerald-and-platinum job that cost something like twenty-two thousand, so she coaxed and pleaded and said how could I be so selfish? And no one would ever know she'd paid for it, and she could boast to her friends how generous I was."

"Oh dear," Valerie said, her sigh sympathetic as she began to understand. "And how would a woman like that consent to come here on a chartered ketch for a honeymoon?"

It was such a good question that Maxwell chuckled softly and squeezed her hand.

"That was part of the prenuptial pact. I'd been brought

up with small boats and I was determined my honeymoon would give me at least a week doing what I'd always wanted to do. I had been thinking of a charter out of the Virgins or Bahamas and then I heard about the Grenadines and I had the money to pay for it. To get her to agree, I had to go along with the emerald ring and consent to move into her Brookline home"—this chuckle had overtones of bitterness—"for the time being."

"Did you ever find out what happened to the first two husbands?"

"Oh, yes. When I began to realize what she was really like, I asked questions here and there. The first one was a big, good-looking ex-Ivy League football player who'd had a fling at pro ball. A lot of muscle and vitality and not much between the ears. When she pushed too far one night, when he couldn't take it any more, he took direct action. I mean, he really gave her a beating.

"Because she was afraid the truth would come out, she didn't press charges in spite of some loose teeth and two broken ribs. To her it was no problem to get into a private hospital until she healed. A week later the husband was out of his job as a customer's man in a local brokerage house. When he tried to move to some other firm, he found there were no openings. A little later he left town: nobody knows where."

He glanced at her and took her hand again, already feeling better as he got things off his chest. "More?" he asked.

"Oh, yes. Please, Alan. You can't stop now."

"The second was a nice guy from a good family. He had the looks and all the social graces, but apparently not much ambition. Mostly he played golf—he had a two handicap and once won the state amateur—and played gin rummy and did some drinking. From what I got, she turned him into a real lush. But with all that booze came impotence, as it usually does. I don't know why, because it was hushed up, and I can only guess it was because she taunted him until he could no longer take it. Anyway, they found him one morning with a nearly empty whisky bottle and an equally empty seconal container.

"The story she gave me before we were married was quite different, and I was perfectly willing to accept her version. She simply had to call the shots. That's the way it had always been, and she had no capacity for change. It didn't matter whether it was instant sexual gratification or the immediate acceptance of any whim or impulse that might come to her.

"She had a habit of tossing a drink in my face. It made little difference where we were—home, at some party, a nightclub," he added, as the memories came flooding back. "Other times it would be a simple slap in the mouth, so I got the habit of grabbing her wrists and holding her after the first slap. Then I guess what happened to the ex-footballer happened to me one night."

Valerie repeated an earlier phrase: "Oh, dear." When he glanced at her she was watching him with a little smile that had an impish quality. "You beat her up."

Maxwell laughed, surprised that he could.

"No. I damn near got myself killed."

"You *what?*"

"We'd come home from some late party both a little mulled. We had an upstairs suite and were in the living room, and we had some words and she threw the drink in my face again. This time there was a change of routine. Maybe it was a reflex action on my part, maybe it was a sense of outrage that had been building for too long; whatever the reason, I had a drink in my hand too, so I threw it back at her.

"When she slapped me and wound up for the second swing, I let her have it—not with a fist, flat-handed across the cheek, but hard enough to knock her down . . . You know, she didn't say a word. She rolled to one knee, and then her feet, and started running into the bedroom, and when she charged back through the doorway she had this little gun in her hand."

He took a deep breath and shook his head absently, as he relived the moment.

"I was shocked enough to be paralyzed, but fortunately something happened. For once I did the right thing. I knew better than to argue or reason with her and the panic took over and I never moved faster in my life. I knew somehow she was going to shoot and I dived for the hall door, swerving, going down in sort of a rolling block as the first two shots came; then scrambling for the doorway, hunched and still weaving. I heard the third slug smack the doorframe and then I was through and sprinting for the head of the stairs.

"Luckily it was not the straight kind, but went down about five steps to a landing and then right-angled the rest of the way. She got off one more shot as I hit the landing and then I was out of sight and vaulting over the bannister. She didn't try to follow; it wouldn't have done her any good. She just stood there screaming her head off until she ran out of breath."

He told Valerie how he'd gone out the back way and walked the streets until he could find a taxi to take him to the University Club, where he'd bought a toothbrush and borrowed a shaving kit. When he'd gone to the office the next afternoon he found he no longer had a job . . .

He put the car in gear and rolled up the drive to the front steps of the hall, and Valerie, as though sensing that he would finish when he was ready, did not prompt him.

"I don't say it was Louise's doing," he said, "although she carried enough weight to make it happen. The senior partner explained it very logically. There was a recession on, defense orders off, everyone curtailing. Engineers, scientists, Ph.D.'s, you name it, were being let go. Our business was off some and the boss said they had to retrench for a while. If I hadn't found something when things picked up, they'd want me back; meanwhile they'd give me the best references and good luck, Alan."

He cut the motor and turned to face her, a slow grin beginning to show. "But things are never all bad," he said, "and I learned then to believe in coincidence. The same morning, before I got to the office, a cable had come from George Osborne saying the ketch was for sale. I'd asked about it when we were on our honeymoon. It was nothing but a wild dream at the time, but I'd told him if he ever wanted to sell it, to let me know. It was the sort of thing people say from time to time and, like that, there was my chance to get out of town and out of the country and do something I'd always wanted to do. I had some insurance money from my father's estate and a month's salary, and the next afternoon, when Louise was at the beauty parlor, I sneaked back, packed two bags, and took off."

He reached for her hand again, the grin broadening. "Now you tell me something. You didn't know I was an architect those first few dates we had, or even that I had a profession; just what did you think I was?"

"Oh," she said lightly, half-closing one eye. "I guess I thought you were a very nice, engaging, beach-bum sort without too much ambition. Although I suppose it had occurred to me that you might be running away from something."

What she did then so surprised him that he reacted tardily. She put both palms alongside his cheeks, turned his face toward her, kissed his mouth warmly and emphatically, and was out of the front seat before he could move. She opened the rear door, got her bags, slammed it, and stuck her head in the lowered window.

"You'll be seeing your wife later?"

"Right now." Maxwell said, still tingling from the kiss. "Dinner tomorrow night?"

"By command performance."

"Oh? Whose?"

"Mother's. By way of celebrating the sale of Bastique tomorrow, I suppose. Just us and the Osbornes and Albert Carswell. If what you say about my fool brother is true, it will be interesting to see what he does about your wife, don't you think?"

5

THE VILLA INN had once been the home of a former resident, a two-story weathered coral structure of at least twelve rooms. With its sale, the inside had been extensively remodeled and two wings and a small swimming pool added. Four small cottages had been built later, two on each side, enabling the establishment to accommodate twenty couples. Standing on a small headland perhaps fifty feet above the shore, it provided an excellent view of the harbor on the right and the approaches to the Aquatic Club and Young's Island on the left. For those who did not like swimming in a pool there was a tiny cove below, one of the few on the island with a decent beach and water free of sea eggs.

The lobby, or lounge and reception desk, was open along the front. Just beyond was the dining room with a small dance floor, and at the far end a patio and pool built close to the edge of the bluff. Now, having been told Mrs. Maxwell had been assigned bungalow No. 4, Maxwell moved along the winding path to the second cottage on the left.

With the sun almost down, dusk was fingering the foliage, and he could see that the lights were on beyond the high slitlike window at one side and the louvered glass door. He knocked once, and stepped inside as a remembered voice called: "Come in!"

Louise Maxwell, formerly Browning, Simpson, and Lathrop, was a small dark-haired woman of twenty-nine. Perhaps five foot two and weighing a hundred and five pounds, she had a full, contoured body and an off-white ivory complexion that gave her an exotic look. The large, artfully shadowed eyes that looked black from a distance were, upon close inspection, an unusual violet.

Noting at once that the man he knew as Leon Carr was sitting languidly in a cushioned chair, Maxwell watched his wife uncurl her tanned bare legs and come to a sitting position on the couch by the wall.

"Well, hello, darling," she said in the low throaty voice she used when things pleased her. "I've been wondering when you'd stop by . . . sit down. Have a drink . . . Leon, ask our guest what he'd like."

"Sugarcane brandy," Maxwell said, knowing she wouldn't have it.

Carr eased out of his chair, turning to the coffee table with its tray of bottles and ice bucket. "Sorry, pal," he said. "Scotch, rum, or vodka."

Maxwell said he'd have Scotch and sat down to watch the drink being fixed, leaning back as he studied the man: in his late thirties, he thought, tall, well proportioned, but with some softness beginning to show in the face and around the waist. He had a lot of medium blond hair and exaggerated sideburns and pale eyes that, almost never direct and seldom still, seemed too small for the face. There was an air of easy insolence about him, and somehow a spurious air of self-importance. Altogether, a man very easy to dislike.

Maxwell took a swallow of his drink, put the glass down, and reached for a cigarette.

"I take it," he said, "you knew I was in town."

"Oh, yes. As a matter of fact we saw you come in. Leon pointed out your boat and then I remembered it."

Maxwell caught the "we," and that brought back what George Osborne had said about Carr and his cameras. This in turn recalled the odd but definite premonition he had ignored earlier as the *Annabel* was coasting to her mooring, and he realized it must have been Carr who had photographed the development plans for Bastique that no one was supposed to know about.

But for what purpose?

The thought bothered him, and he decided not to mention it.

"What took you so long to find me, Louise?"

"Actually I didn't start to look until a bit more than a month ago."

"Why?"

"Why did I wait?" Her quick smile was sly, the eyes veiled. "Or why did I take the trouble to come at all?"

"Both."

"Let's say I couldn't be bothered at first. I had no idea where you'd disappeared to. There was no particular hurry about a divorce. I could always find an attractive escort somewhere along the way and being a married woman had certain advantages."

She finished her drink and waved the glass at Carr, who jumped to refill it.

"Or maybe I thought it would be fun to let you make the first move. I suppose, when time went by and nothing happened, I began to get annoyed. A couple of months ago I decided to do something about it."

"Because you couldn't stand a man, any man, walking out on you?"

"Something like that," she said, and there was a sudden chill in the room. "I had to kick my first husband out," she added, mouth tightening in the old familiar way. "The second was an impotent weakling with a lot of charm and no backbone. What he did to himself was bound to happen sooner or later."

"Then I was sort of in between," Maxwell said, reaching for his glass. "I didn't beat you up, I didn't kill myself; I simply ran out on you while I still had my health. But no one does that to Louise and gets away with it, right?"

"Quite."

"I see you're still wearing your engagement ring."

"Oh, yes." She held up her left hand, turning it so the facets and prisms of the emerald could best catch the light. "I love it . . . perhaps because it so reminds me of you," she added with studied sarcasm. "I suppose you talked to George Osborne?"

"I have."

"He gave you the news? . . . Yes, I see by your cute scowl that he must have. But darling, you're not to blame the poor man. He didn't dream he was assigning the mortgage or papers or whatever to a scheming vindictive bitch who was only out to make trouble for you. He thought I was a repentant, remorseful wife who only wanted to surprise you with an unexpected gift."

"So he told me." Maxwell stood up and finished his drink in an effort to wash the disgust from his throat. "I imagine you have some plans."

"Nothing definite." She was smiling again, apparently enjoying herself thoroughly. "I thought perhaps Monday I'd have a talk with your barrister friend—Carswell, isn't it?—and see about getting a court order to lock you out and tie your boat up temporarily."

"If you can."

"And why can't I?"

"Maybe you can in the end, but I still may have a chance because Osborne found out what you're really like before he cashed your check. He still has it. Until he does, the court may rule that the assignment isn't final."

"You intend to take it to court?" The painted mouth

tightened and the laugh that followed was abrupt and derisive.

"You can count on it. Down here you're in *my* backyard, sweetheart. They might rule in my favor, you know. And while the judge is making up his mind he might just let me have the continued use of the boat."

"That might be fun, seeing you in court." She stood up, smoothed the shorts over her hips and arched her back like a cat stretching. The white blouse stretched briefly across her breasts to outline the nipples and let him know she wore no brassiere. "Now, you'd better run along, darling. You too, Leon. I have to change."

Carr, who had been listening to the exchange in amused silence, eased up out of his chair and hitched his yellow slacks over the bulging waistline. He took his time finishing his drink, his smile working as he glanced from Maxwell to the woman.

"Anything I can do? What about tomorrow?"

"I'll let you know," she said, not bothering to look at him. She had moved close to Maxwell, the violet eyes that looked up at him challenging and sardonic. "I expect I'll see you tomorrow at three, Alan."

"Three?" Maxwell watched her narrowly, annoyed that he should sound so stupid but not quite understanding.

"Why, yes. Isn't that when Bastique is supposed to be sold?"

He felt the points of her breasts touch lightly the front of his shirt and stood his ground, his thoughts confused as some strange sense of dismay began to build inside him. To avoid her glance and gain a little time he deliberately examined the room.

Like any large American motel room, but longer from front to back so that, undivided, it comprised two areas. The front half by the door and wide picture window with its sea view, had the sofa, wicker chairs with cushions, odd lamps, and native-built occasional tables. Twin beds and chests made up the rear, with an added bath that was not only good-sized but boasted that rarity on the island, a tub.

Aware of his self-created silence and still battling his suspicions, he said, "So I understand. Were you invited?"

"Certainly, darling." She put one hand up to pat his cheek as a forgiving mother might do to a wayward child. The gesture was so familiar, and at the moment so repugnant, that he drew his head back sharply to leave her hand suspended in mid-air and saw then the quick glints of fury in her eyes. Now, stepping back, she added, her tone brittle and triumphant: "By Michael Atherton. Or hadn't you heard about us?"

He wheeled quickly then, no longer trusting his self-control. Her brittle laugh followed him out the door and with it came some new stirring of alarm as his imagination began to feed on the possibility that something might happen to spoil the Bastique deal and his chance to re-establish himself in his profession.

Still trying to scoff at this new feeling of doubt and uncertainty, he was aware that Leon Carr was keeping pace as they went up the path to the main entrance. Here he stopped abruptly to face the other, his wide mouth grim and his eyes smouldering.

"They tell me," he said tightly, "you've been snooping around the Casurina Inn."

"I have?" Carr said blandly.

"You were seen going into my room," he added, the lie coming easily.

"Who by?"

"One of the help."

"If I was and you objected you'd be preferring charges instead of running off at the mouth, wouldn't you? . . . She got under your skin, hunh?" He grunted softly, mouth twisting. "It's a thing she knows how to do."

"You work for her?"

"Sure. For a month now. And get well paid. I do what I can, so forget it," he said, putting a hand on Maxwell's shoulder. "Come on, I'll buy you a drink."

Maxwell shrugged the hand aside, annoyed with himself for his lack of self-control and wanting only to get away from there.

6

THE MORNING FLIGHT FROM BARBADOS was on time and Alan Maxwell watched from the visitors' enclosure as the engines were cut and the loading ramp locked into place. Alongside him, Albert Carswell wore a freshly laundered white drill suit and a stained felt hat that looked like some relic of better days.

Sam Blake's request for reservations mentioned a party of four and he was one of the first off, suggesting that he had traveled first class. Even so, Maxwell could not identify Blake's companions until they stood apart and he saw then a younger, taller, black-haired man and two still-younger girls who looked most attractive in their short bright summer dresses. When he caught Blake's eye he pointed to the "Arrivals" doorway and then went round to the front. There a blue-uniformed Negro police sergeant with a swagger stick was keeping an eye on the proceedings as if to make sure the customs and immigration formalities were properly completed.

Outside, Blake, a stout but not yet fat man with a round florid face and not much hair on the top of his head, shook hands with Maxwell and Carswell. Shrewd observant dark eyes suggested not only a quick and capable brain but a core of inner hardness. His outward air of breezy affability fooled no one who knew him and seemed only a cover for a businesslike, no-nonsense manner.

"Tony Russo—Alan Maxwell, Albert Carswell," he said, indicating the slender, flat-muscled man with swart skin, a small mustache, and a lean expressionless face. With the two girls he was less formal, and it was not until some time later that Maxwell knew they had last names. For the present, the redhead was Agnes and the platinum blonde was Elsie. They were about the same height and had straight hair somewhat below shoulder length; Agnes offered perhaps an inch more in the three measurements most often used in judging the female form, but both were shapely, with bright empty faces and artificial smiles.

Now, as the porter deposited their baggage on the paving, Blake said: "You got our reservations?"

"All set."

"Transportation?"

Maxwell pointed to his Consul and Carswell's Morris. He supervised the porter in loading the bags and Blake arranged the seating.

"You girls ride with Carswell," he said. "Tony and I'll go with Alan. Okay, let's go. It's past time for a drink."

On the ride to the inn, Blake avoided the subject that had brought him here, and when they had collected in front of the reception desk he again took charge.

"You register for us, Tony. You go along with the boys, girls"—he indicated the two bellboys who were lining up the bags—"and get unpacked."

"Can we change into our swimsuits?" Agnes asked.

"Sure, anything you like. I'll be around somewhere but don't bother me. I've got business on my mind." He turned to Carswell and dismissed him forthwith. "Albert, we'll see you at the Atherton place at three, right? And don't be late."

For a second or two Carswell's sad eyes looked hurt but

he recovered quickly and his tone remained polite and courteous.

"Of course, Mr. Blake. I'll have everything we need on hand. I assume you have a certified check."

"I sure have, Albert," Blake said and took Maxwell by the arm, leading him through the dining room, signaling to the barman as he passed, and selecting a table in the shade at the near end of the pool.

"What'll you have?" he said when the barman came.

"Francis knows," Maxwell said, and Francis said, "Yes, sir, Mr. Maxwell. Sugarcane brandy and soda."

Blake asked if Francis had any bourbon and when the barman said yes, he said, "On the rocks, Francis, with a touch of water."

"Some view," he said, as he leaned back to wait for the drinks. "And what a climate . . . Everything under control?"

"So far as I know," Maxwell said, seeing no reason to mention the thumbtack holes or his suspicions.

"The Athertons don't know about our plans for a complete island development?"

"I don't see how."

When the drinks came Blake took a grateful swallow, said, "Ahh—" and as he leaned back once more and stretched his legs Maxwell's thoughts reverted to their first meeting more than a year before . . .

He had been between charters when Blake arrived on the island unannounced, along with a tall, strongly built man named Thompson, who, it turned out, was a construction engineer. They had come to Maxwell because his was the most comfortable boat available and money seemed no object.

They had gone to Bastique under sail in one long reach, just squeezing by the northeast headland at Bequia but staying well to the west of Baliceaux. Approaching Bastique they had gone under power so they could completely circumnavigate the island before anchoring in the lagoon. He had put them ashore in the dinghy, and they had been gone most of the day. They had given no real indication of what they had in mind, but Maxwell had begun to get an idea of his own.

For he had heard that Bastique had been offered for sale at various times in the past. As he understood it, the reason it had not yet been sold was simple enough. A figure would be set by the owners, but each time a bona fide offer was made a family conference would result in some stalemate or difference of opinion, and the price would be revised upward. More recently, the improving travel facilities, especially from the States, had brought increasing numbers of tourists, and all land values throughout the Grenadines, but particularly St. Vincent and Bequia, had been increasing as off-islanders began to buy up small parcels and make investments.

At no time did Blake or Thompson reveal their interest; but when they came ashore in the late afternoon they asked if he could recommend a reliable attorney. Maxwell, knowing Carswell's efforts to sell the island, had referred them to him.

Some months later a letter and a check from Blake had requested a week's charter. As before, he arrived with Thompson, but on the following day, while they were anchored in the lagoon, a float plane winged up from Trinidad with a surveyor and rodman. All that day and the next they stayed at work, and it was that third evening after the plane had departed that Maxwell got the break he had been waiting for.

Blake and Thompson were having a nightcap in the main cabin. Oscar Jones was asleep in his bunk when Maxwell came up through the forward hatch in his shorts to get some air and have a last smoke. He was sitting on the cabin trunk and the voices were coming distinctly through the two open rectangular ports. Minutes later the words he heard took form and substance and he acted at once, hurrying back to the bow cabin, donning slacks, sneakers, and a shirt. Ducking down the small companionway he paused only long enough to knock and then he was inside and talking fast, explaining how he had happened to be topside and what he had heard.

"I didn't mean to eavesdrop," he said. "I mean, at first. After I got the gist of what you were saying I listened deliberately."

They looked at him then as though aware for the first time that he might be something more than a charter-boat captain. They exchanged glances and Blake put down his glass.

"Oh, why?"

"You plan to have an inn and some cottages—assuming that you buy the island?"

"So?"

"You'll need an architect."

"So?"

"Have you got one?"

"Not yet."

"Then it would be an advantage, wouldn't it, and probably cheaper, to have an architect right here on the ground floor rather than import one? Someone who knows the people and how to get along with them, and just what's available in the way of manpower and materials."

Thompson got it first. "You're an architect? With a degree?"

"From Cornell. You're from Boston?"

"We are."

"If you're in the construction business you should have heard of Richardson, Chapman and Watson."

"You were with them?"

"Sort of junior-junior partner until I got surplused, as they used to say."

"Surplused?" Blake frowned, still unconvinced.

"Laid off like a thousand others that worked for the electronics boys along Route 128. When Mr. Richardson gave me the bad news he said he'd give me a top reference. You could write him, or give him a ring when you get back."

By that time Thompson was nodding. "It's a top firm, Sam—But let me ask you this, Maxwell," he added. "What makes you think you could handle a resort inn?"

"I designed and supervised that Nationwide Motel down near Foxboro. A proper kitchen efficiently laid out, dining room, sleeping rooms—what's the difference? However—"

He paused here, purposely.

"However what?" Blake said, taking the gambit.

"If I'm to be considered for the job, I'd like to make a suggestion."

"All right. For what it's worth, you're considered."

"You plan to remodel and enlarge The Residence and add maybe six cottages, right?"

"Go on."

"I think you're making a serious mistake."

Blake sat up, florid face clouding. "Wait a minute!" he said with some resentment.

"Easy, Sam," Thompson said, his tone amused. "Let's hear the lad out. Why, Maxwell? Why are we making a mistake?"

"For two chief reasons," Maxwell said, determined now to take the risk and gamble that he could convince them.

"Go on," Thompson said.

"Before I do I might have a couple of thoughts on the plus side. First, you'll get a big tax break for the first ten years—"

"We already know about that."

"—and your biggest expenses—fixtures, hardware, plumbing, kitchen equipment, and appliances—can come in duty-free on any new hotel. Bastique is under St. Vincent's

jurisdiction and this is just one of the government's induce-
ments to promote hotel construction."

He saw from the quick exchange of glances that he had
scored, and he felt a pleasant sense of accomplishment in
being able to bring out a point they had apparently overlooked.

Thompson nodded and half-closed one eye as he regarded his companion. "That's a bonus we hadn't figured
on," he said finally. "So what're these objections you seem
so sure of? Two, you said? Let's take number one."

"I've been in The Residence," Maxwell said. "It's solid
enough but it only has six bedrooms and one bath. You're
talking about eighteen or twenty rooms, according to what
I overheard. That means, these days, twenty baths. You
need a complete and modern kitchen, hardware, fixtures,
furniture. Lump these items together and you'll lay out
more money than the actual construction will come to and
you'll have a hybrid structure. In any case, when you're
ready to open you're going to need help. Where is the
help going to stay? They can't commute—"

"Ahh," Thompson said, some new interest showing in his
glance. "What you're saying is that it will cost us about as
much to build a new inn as to remodel. Instead of provid-
ing additional quarters for the help, use The Residence
about as it is."

"Something like that. Equipment is your big cost, because every bit of it has to be imported. Labor, your biggest cost at home, is cheap."

Blake, not yet convinced, said, "What about the native
families on the island that already live right here?"

"You'll get a little day labor, sure, but—"

Again Thompson interrupted. "Hold on. You may have
something." He hesitated, eyes still half-closed but busy.
"You said two reasons, what's the other one?"

"If you remodel and build cottages you'll be putting

them in the wrong place. That's the weather shore. You'll have just one tiny cove for safe sea bathing. In or near the south shore or lagoon the wind won't blow the hair off your guests and the pictures off the walls. You'll have all the safe sandy beach you can use . . ."

He glanced up, thoughts jerking back to the present as Tony Russo pulled out a chair and sat down. He had discarded his jacket and tie and opened the top buttons of his shirt. He had what looked like a rum punch with its coating of nutmeg in one hand, and a cigarette in his thin mouth. When Blake took no notice of him Maxwell finished the mental sequence that had become so familiar in recent months.

Actually, from the moment he had gained the construction engineer's interest and respect, the rest had been comparatively easy. The first thing Blake wanted to know once he began to consider Maxwell's suggestions seriously, was how far he could go on a speculative basis.

"Preliminary sketches. Perspectives and front and side elevations."

When Thompson asked, "What have you got to lose, Sam?" Blake said, "How long?"

"Two weeks."

"We'll check you out with your old firm. You send your sketches along. We'll let you know."

There had been no further questions about his ideas or abilities. Because, just as a mechanic takes his tool chest wherever he goes, Maxwell had brought his case of drawing instruments, and all he needed was paper and ink. The sketches were in the mail on time, and a month later he had received a check for $1,500 along with a request for rough layouts—not detailed working drawings but his conception of the overall design, showing the location of the kitchen, public rooms, and suggested floor plan . . .

The scraping of Blake's chair as he finally turned his back on the view cut Maxwell's train of thought in time for him to hear the other say, "What was the name of that barman?"

"Francis."

Blake called out and held up his glass. Then, abruptly and with no prologue, he said, "So what do you think about the material we mailed you a while ago?"

"If you mean the overall development plan, I think it's great, but who's going to design and oversee the building of the golf course?"

"We've got a man. From our contour maps and surveys he had enough for a rough layout. You know—yardages, green placements. We even got an estimate of probable costs. He says we won't have to water anything except the greens; no underground stuff. No blasting and rock hauling like at home. No heavy power equipment. He made inquiries on labor costs, and he thinks we can do the whole eighteen for a couple hundred thousand against four hundred thousand plus exclusive of land, in our area. When it's completed it will be the best damn layout south of Puerto Rico."

He went on with details after his drink came, and Maxwell watched Tony Russo give Francis his empty glass and a silent order. Still only half-listening, he found part of his mind wondering about this man Sam Blake had brought with him.

On receiving the $1,500, he had written to the one friend in Boston who knew where he was and could be trusted to keep the information to himself. A young lawyer with a good firm, he had done a little research when Maxwell had asked him to find out what he could about the Island Development Company and a Samuel Blake.

The report had been good. The company was a going concern, well rated in Dun and Bradstreet and with competent management, Blake being the New England representative. Its stock was listed on the over-the-counter market and reasonably active. There were unconfirmed reports that the original capital had come from Syndicate money, but any such ownership was not evident.

Now, watching Russo, Maxwell found himself wondering just what his function was. His tight angular face seemed at all times impassive. The flat opaque eyes seemed empty of either compassion or emotion, so that he was able to maintain an air of studied indifference and still remind you that he was fully aware of what was being said and would be available in whatever capacity he might be needed.

He had spoken not one word to Maxwell, nor did he bother to look at him now as Blake, his dissertation finished, glanced at his watch.

"Where are the girls?"

"On the beach. They couldn't wait to get out of their clothes."

"Let them know we'll have some lunch in an hour. What about you, Alan? Care to join us? They're a couple of great kids."

"Thanks, but I have to change." He stood up, and another thought came to him. "That is, if you want me along. Actually there's no real reason why—"

"No, no," Blake cut in. "You're friendly with all the Athertons. You can be our liaison man. Why don't you pick us up around two-thirty, and we'll get it over with."

Maxwell said fine. He glanced at Russo, but when he saw that the man had no intention of acknowledging his departure, he wheeled and walked away.

7

HARDIN HALL WAS A BLOCKY, solid-looking structure of gray, weathered coral. Two-storied throughout, the center part was square, with the two wings set slightly back. The drive, lined most of the way with casurina trees bent gracefully and permanently by the prevailing winds, was a good quarter of a mile long. In the rear and hidden from the drive were a lawn, a paved patio, a grass tennis court, and a swimming pool.

Apparently this transaction was to take place in the house, because as Alan Maxwell parked, the massive front door opened and Valerie Atherton came out to greet them. She was wearing a simple off-white dress this time, with a skirt length similar to the navy suit he had seen yesterday, the well-formed thighs somewhat more in evidence when viewed from the lower angle. Again the feather cut was slightly windblown, but her smile was genuine as she shook hands with Blake and was introduced to Russo, who, as was his custom, nodded and said nothing.

"You're right on time," she said. "Come in. Mother's waiting inside with Albert Carswell."

They followed her into the wide half-light of the hall and on through the doorway at the right to a long, high-

ceilinged room, furnished mostly with heavy, dark furniture that looked as if it had been a long time in the family.
The orientals were authentic and the wide floorboards
where visible, held a high polish. Albert Carswell, who was
sitting next to Dorothy at a round tip-top table, came to
his feet. Michael Atherton, who had been sitting next to
Louise Maxwell on the divan, did the same.

Blake went directly to Dorothy Atherton, who offered
her hand. He did not bother to introduce Russo, who slid
into a chair well off to one side. When Maxwell introduced
Blake to his wife, Blake gave her a long, appraising glance
that revealed nothing. Albert Carswell, very neat in his
old-fashioned white suit, busied himself with the papers on
the round table.

"I have your check here, Mrs. Atherton," Blake said.
"Shall we get on with it?"

The woman sat very straight on the divan, and took
some time with her reply. Maxwell could tell something
was bothering her greatly. Her handsome face, always
dignified, seemed tense at the mouth and jaw, her expression unusually severe. She was a big-boned woman,
strongly built, as tall as he was and weighing better than
a hundred and fifty pounds but, in late middle age, still
shapely.

With her deep blue eyes and white hair, parted and
pulled loosely back to a bun, she was a striking-looking
woman, active, vital. She dressed more often than not in
jodhpurs and spent most of her days riding in the fields
and haranguing the workers. Strong-willed and determined,
she had gained a benevolent dominance over her son just
as she had with her husband, who, to all accounts, had
been a gentle, ineffectual man. Only Valerie and the doctor
son, Ian, in England, had escaped this influence. That
Michael should, in such a short time, defy her in his infatuation with Louise was quite beyond her comprehension.

"I'm afraid," she said finally, "there have been complications."

"Complications?" Blake scowled at the room as though expecting some attack on his flank. "How, Mrs. Atherton? We have a deal, a legal option, and the right to exercise it up until midnight Monday."

"Albert!" She looked at Carswell, commanding him to explain.

"I'm afraid she refers to a certain clause," he said unhappily, "which states that if at any time during the life of that option a completely unsolicited offer should be made in excess of yours, the family has a right to accept it. If such an offer is met by you, the right to purchase remains yours."

Blake's florid face was clouding as his mouth tightened, obliterating his air of breezy affability.

"You're saying that such an offer has been made?"

"I'm afraid it has."

"How much?"

"Four hundred thousand."

"By whom?"

"By me," a new voice said, and Maxwell had to glance round to realize the statement had come from his wife.

With it came a few seconds of profound silence and Maxwell could only stare at her, his immediate thoughts confused and a little panicky. Blake recovered first.

"You have a certified check with you?"

"I have already established credit in that amount, with the local branch of Barclay's Bank. Would you like to phone the manager?"

Maxwell knew she wasn't bluffing; so, apparently, did Blake. Before he could reply Dorothy Atherton spoke, her voice frigid but still controlled.

"We learned today of certain plans of yours, Mr. Blake, that must have been a rather well-kept secret. Show him, Albert!"

It was then that Maxwell noticed an object on the round table that had been partly hidden by the various papers. He saw now that it was a hand slide-viewer with a long focal length and a thick lens. Carswell also picked up four or five film clips and passed them to Blake.

Maxwell knew instantly, and with a growing dismay, exactly what they were. Leon Carr and his cameras. The thumbtack holes in the Bastique maps, blueprints, and overlays. Now he watched trancelike while Blake fitted the first bit of film into the viewer. He tried another, a curious hardness beginning to show around the jaw. He continued to ignore the others in the room until he had finished. He put them aside, glanced at Russo, and then back at Dorothy Atherton.

"Where did these come from?"

"She"—she pointed at Louise—"provided them."

"How did you get them, Mrs. Maxwell?"

"I don't see that it's any of your business, Mr. Blake," Louise said flatly, and the quick angling look she gave Maxwell seemed to carry a gleam of triumph.

The smugness of that look, the sharp and bitter memory of other times when she had worn it in the past, infuriated him and he spoke to Blake of the discovery he had made on his return from Grenada the previous afternoon. He said it seemed obvious now that his wife had hired Leon Carr in Boston not only to locate him but to gather every possible bit of information about his present activities.

"I don't think Carr was searching my room for anything in particular. He was just doing a job. Photographing the maps and prints when he found them was just routine."

Somewhere a throat was cleared, and Tony Russo made his first contribution.

"I know Carr, Sam," he said. "He's a licensed snoop back home, and if he's in town Maxwell probably has it pegged. When I see Carr I'll make sure."

"The fact remains, Mr. Blake"—Dorothy Atherton had listened long enough and, as usual, came right to the heart of the matter—"you misled us about your intended use of Bastique. We were assured that you proposed to construct a resort-type inn and cottages."

"We still do," Blake said, "but even the fine print doesn't limit us to that."

"Hundreds of lots—" she began, as though such a projection were beyond her comprehension.

"Six hundred and four, to be exact."

"—and a golf course," she finished. "A purely commercial venture."

"So?" Blake said, "What is it, hallowed ground?" He waved a hand at Louise. "Just what do you propose to do with it?"

"We haven't decided, not definitely."

"Who's we?"

"Michael and I." She smiled at young Atherton and he smiled back, content, it seemed, to maintain his silence. "My thought was to leave the island as it is except for The Residence. I'd love to restore it, add some baths and a proper power plant. It will make an ideal place to come for a few weeks in the winter, or whenever Michael wants to visit."

It took a few seconds for Dorothy to recover from what was obviously unexpected and shocking news. Her tone was outraged.

"*Michael!* How can you be childish enough even to think about marriage with a woman who already has a husband? Are you out of your mind?"

Atherton stared right back at his mother, defiance showing in his eyes as he let Louise answer.

"This woman," she said smugly, "won't have a husband long. With Alan's consent, it can be arranged in a few days in Mexico. Without it, I'll simply establish residence in

Nevada. The only way he can stop me is to appear personally and contest my petition, which I doubt he'll want to do."

"Look!" Blake demanded attention, and his flat hard tone got it. "I'm not interested in your personal problems; I'm here to buy an island, so let's get on with it. You're saying I have to get up another thirty thousand by Monday midnight. Okay. There's still time today to get in touch with my people. They'll fly someone down by Monday with the cash."

"That may not be enough."

It was Michael Atherton's turn to talk and Maxwell watched with growing bewilderment as he patted Louise's knee and stood up. He was tall like his mother, his eyes the same shade of blue but without the same intensity. His wavy blond hair was shaggy, and there was a line across his forehead where his workday pith helmet had left its mark. He had an easy smile and manner but little of his mother's drive and determination. Now Maxwell saw the stubborn angle of the jaw and understood that for once he was daring her to challenge him.

Again it was Blake who replied. "What the hell do you mean?" he demanded, no longer caring for the amenities. "You signed that option and you're stuck with it."

"There are four of us with votes. I have my brother's power of attorney, a proxy if you like."

"The one in London, the doctor? And you're going to vote him against us?" He glanced at Valerie. "How about you, Miss Atherton? You signed in good faith."

Valerie had been sitting quite still, hands in her lap and a puzzled frown working on the smoothness of her skin. When she realized Blake was waiting, she gave Maxwell a tentative smile.

"Yes," she said. "I think this haggling and Michael's silly attempt to please a woman he's known less than a week is downright dishonest."

"You, Mrs. Atherton?" Blake asked quietly.

The woman nodded silently, her eyes still on her son, and traces of shock, censure, and something akin to despair in their depths.

"Okay," Blake said, his tone suggesting that the matter was settled. "We'll get in touch with that doctor son, whatever his name is. A power of attorney can be nullified in a hurry if you know how. A little pressure of one kind or another."

"We've still got three days, Sam," Russo said as if they were now on a subject he understood. "Lots of things could happen."

Louise answered with a quick affected laugh. "Is that a threat of some kind, Mr. Russo?"

Russo's flat expressionless eyes examined her across the room. A thin smile flattened the mustache. It stayed fixed and humorless as he considered Michael briefly.

"You know what I mean," he said in the same even monotone. "Who can say we'll all be here Monday? People fall over from heart attacks every day, some as young as you are. They have traffic accidents, or get run over—"

"Please."

It was Carswell this time, and Maxwell saw the distress in the tired features. Having listened to these unexpected complications he seemed appalled at the thought that his future might be crumbling about him. He had come to his feet and his mouth trembled as he fought for words. Maxwell knew exactly how he felt, for he understood only too well that his own future was in some doubt.

"Please don't talk nonsense, Michael. If you persist this whole matter will wind up in the courts. It would drag on for months, years. Years," he said again, almost in tears. "That's how long I've worked to sell Bastique. What about my commission?"

"Commission?" Dorothy Atherton seemed to rouse herself from her moment of weakness, and her tone was once

again businesslike and practical. "What about your commission, Albert? You know the terms of our agreement. If
Bastique is sold through your efforts you are to have five
percent. If, on the other hand, the buyer should be someone who approached us voluntarily there would be no
commission involved. Expenses, of course. Perhaps a token
payment, but without obligation on our part. I'm sure you
are aware—"

"Yes, but—" Carswell got this much out, but then the
thoughts of possible failure overwhelmed him and he gave
up.

With that, Blake came to his feet. "We'll be here Monday with the extra thirty thousand, Mrs. Atherton. We'll
expect to close the deal then on the terms of our original
agreement." He looked at Michael and took pains with his
words. "Think it over good, son . . . Come on, Tony—Alan."

In the silence that followed, Maxwell caught Valerie's
eye and signaled her with a tip of his head. She nodded
and rose to follow him. In the hall he called ahead to
Blake to say he'd be with him in a minute.

"What a mess."

She nodded, the green eyes inspecting him and her
half-smile twisted. She took a deep breath, the front of her
dress showing some strain, and exhaled noisily.

"I wouldn't have believed it if I hadn't seen it. I suppose
it goes to show what a pretty woman with a willing body
can do to some men. But Michael, of all people. He never
really had what you'd call a steady girl. If you asked me
I'd have said he was still a virgin."

"Maybe that's the reason she got to him so easily."

"Well"—she made a face—"he makes me sick. He's going
to get a talking-to about—"

"I wouldn't," Maxwell said and then, with forced cheer-
fulness, "but let's forget it for now."

"All right," she said, and this time a smile came. "I will
if you will."

"What about dinner? Is it still on?"

"Knowing mother, I'd say yes. Once she's made up her mind to do something she's very hard to stop. Short of a death in the family—"

"What time?"

"She said something about leaving here around seven."

A double tap of a horn informed Maxwell of Blake's impatience, so he gave her hand a final squeeze and said he'd pick her up.

8

THE VILLA INN had for some time advertised two evenings of entertainment for its guests and those townsmen who wanted to step out. On Friday a steel band was featured along with a good buffet and perhaps a limbo exhibition at which guests could try their hand squirming beneath the bar. Saturdays a conventional five-piece band played for dancing and featured a calypso singer.

On this particular Friday there was a good turnout but the Atherton table was hardly a festive one. The drinks kept coming prior to the meal, but Dorothy seemed not to feel them, while Albert Carswell's reaction was somewhat the opposite, giving him an air of spurious gaiety that required additional stimulants from time to time.

As was the custom on such occasions—there had been two similar dinners at which Maxwell had been a guest—the hostess dominated the group in all respects. She told everyone where to sit and supervised the subject matter for discussion. There was no limit on drinks, and since Maxwell had never seen a check paid he assumed that she was billed later.

As Valerie had predicted, young Atherton had refused to join the family table and sat near the pool-end of the

room across from Louise Maxwell. For that reason Maxwell, Wanda, and Valerie had been seated with their backs
to the dance floor. Sam Blake and his party had a table on
the opposite side of the room, and Maxwell was unable to
say later who had danced with whom and who had left the
table during the evening, or for how long.

He had danced with Valerie after his hostess had de-
clined his obligatory invitation, and when they had finished their coffee he took Wanda's hand and asked if she
could stand a chorus with him. Because rudeness was
foreign to her nature she stood up, but he sensed her
reluctance and understood the reason for it. Good manners
had compelled her to sit with her back to the one man in
the room who meant anything to her, and pride alone kept
her from displaying any outward sign of the emotions
which must have been torturing her throughout the evening.

She was easy to dance with, and her firm-fleshed body
felt good in his arms. She kept her back straight and her
chin up, her cheek resting lightly against his. His con-
versational gambits sounded as weak and witless in his
ears as her forced responses until he felt her body stiffen
as she caught her breath.

"Look, Alan! Do you think they're quarreling?"

She turned him so he could look over her shoulder as
she spoke and he saw what she meant. The last time he
had glanced at the table for two, Louise and Michael had
been a picture of intimacy, their foreheads almost touching
as they talked; now he saw the woman's expression was
twisted and ugly. He thought he could hear the rising fury
of her voice against the background of the steel band, and
Atherton was sitting open-mouthed and bewildered before
Wanda turned him again so she could observe and relish
the scene . . .

Back at the table, Dorothy Atherton kept the conversation going in a desultory way by the sheer force of her

personality. She tried to divide her time equally between Carswell and Osborne when they weren't at the bar. She brought Wanda into the conversation whenever she could and seemed intent on preventing the girl from turning to watch her son.

At one point Maxwell had noticed Leon Carr at the bar talking with a young local couple; and now some stubborn, nagging impulse that could not be denied demanded that he have one more session alone with Louise. He could not have explained why, and he was at that point in his drinking when such brooding eventually turned into a full-fledged obsession. When, sometime around ten, he glanced over his shoulder to find Michael sitting by himself at the small table and looking quite miserable, he saw his chance.

As if by prearrangement, it was then that Valerie rose to excuse herself. Since it was standard practice for any woman to request female company each time she went to the john, she extended the customary and easily recognizable invitation.

"Wanda?"

The girl managed a tired smile and shook her head. "I'm all right, Val."

Carswell had just come back from somewhere and Osborne had been last seen talking to Carr at the bar. Now, as Carswell leaned forward to address the two women, Maxwell stood up. He made his excuses which nobody heard and then he strolled towards the lobby. The restrooms opened near the front entrance and he hesitated, to see if anyone had noticed him. Satisfied, he slipped outside, turning right and keeping to the shadowed edges of the parking lot until he was on the curving path to the two bungalows on that side.

Lights showed from the windows of the near one, but he could detect no sound from inside. The hammered rhythms of the steel band still dominated the starred blackness of the night, and when he saw a glow from the odd, slitlike window high up in the wall of the second bungalow, he quickened his step. The shadows were thick here from the bordering foliage and because of the light from the first bungalow his eyes were not fully adjusted to the darkness ahead and he moved more by feel than by sight.

For that reason he was never quite sure about some fancied movement just beyond the door of his wife's bungalow. This impression was, however, of sufficient substance to make him check his stride, to make him wonder if he *had* actually seen a moving shadow darker than the rest. For another second he tried to pierce the total blackness beyond the door, but checked the impulse to announce his presence. Uncertain now, he began to wonder if the drinks he'd put away had affected his sight, imagination, or both.

Finally, scoffing at such thoughts, he stumbled toward the pale rectangle of light which came through the pebbled-glass louvers of the door.

He did not bother to knock and when the knob turned freely he pushed inside stubbornly, not caring if Louise liked it or not or whom she might be entertaining, not even quite sure just what he was going to say now that he was here.

The thought, the compulsion to see her, had seemed important enough a couple of drinks ago and would probably come back to him. All he was sure of was one simple resolution—to keep his hands off her no matter how mad she made him.

In that first instant as he stumbled across the threshold and swung the door behind him, he thought the room was empty. The single shaded table lamp seemed only to intensify the remaining shadows and he squinted ahead, puzzled and momentarily uncertain. When he remembered the bathroom he called:

"Louise . . . *Hey, Louise!*"

He pulled himself more stiffly erect, trying to concentrate now but having no premonition yet that anything was wrong. He had taken two steps and swerved round a table just ahead when the rest of the room became visible. It was then that he saw the small still figure on the floor near the foot of the nearest bed.

Some reflex action froze him there. He saw the red dress, the skirt hiked nearly to the hips. Mascaraed lashes obscured the eyes, and the once-pretty face with its cap of black hair seemed slack and gray.

His mental reaction, less swift, left him stunned and empty-headed, his stare uncomprehending. Not yet thinking, he spoke automatically, his voice a hoarse whisper as he bent over her.

"Louise . . . *Louise!*"

He tried to shake her shoulder and found it warm and heavy and unresponsive.

He slid damp fingers down the smooth skin to lift a limp wrist. But by then the shaking had started and he could not tell if there was a pulse or not. He knelt then, putting one ear to her mouth and nose. Not until his fingertips found the neck artery and the frightening stillness there could he accept the fact that his wife was dead.

Not knowing how this could have happened but only that it must have been very recent, he started to lift his head. Only then did he notice the small stain that was much darker than the fabric. No larger than a fifty-cent piece, it was between the breasts and perhaps an inch closer to the left one. The tiny hole centering the stain would have gone unnoticed had he not looked for it.

He pushed to his feet, conscious of the tremor in his knees, his stomach a vacuum. Then, as those first awful shock waves passed, the fear came. He remembered the other time a gun had been used and the panic that had sent him scrambling from that bedroom with bullets chasing him. This fear was different but nonetheless real.

Because he'd had some thought of violence in his mind when he came. He knew that now, just as he knew that when a wife was murdered it was the husband who was at once the chief suspect.

And why not?

Who could have a stronger motive than one who knew, better than anyone, the victim with all her faults and aggravating ways?

In his case it was worse. He'd run from this woman and it was now known that she had pursued him maliciously, intent on taking his boat and then doing her best to ruin the opportunity for a new career and new hope—

He forced an end to such thoughts and found he was breathing regularly again. The trembling had stopped but his mouth and throat were so dry he had to swallow twice. It was at that moment that he heard the odd sound and knew instantly that it came not from the room but from outside.

It was not repeated but it was, to his finely tuned senses, distinct and quite different from the remote beating of the steel band. A sharp, snapping sound like a dry branch breaking close by one wall.

He moved at once, ears still straining and eyes flicking about the interior. No one could see through the pebbled glass door. The drapes on the picture window had been drawn. The long high window opposite was open and had been put at that height to prevent any passing voyeur from indulging his hobby.

Seconds later he was outside, feeling his way along the perimeter of the bungalow until his eyes could adjust to the darkness. Low shrubs and bushes impeded him but he brushed them aside blindly and swore softly because he had no flashlight.

When he had made one complete circuit of the bungalow he stopped again by the closed door, his nerves still ragged and his frustration inhibiting his ability to think clearly. He had already started to reach for the doorknob when something happened and his mental fog lifted. Miraculously, new thoughts began to click in swift succession through his brain, and he had never been more sober in his life.

The first impulse, to go inside and call the police, he discarded forthwith. He knew what would happen. Someone at the inn's switchboard would eventually answer and connect him with police headquarters. At this hour there was no telling who might be in charge. He would be told to stand by, touch nothing, and await the arrival of the law.

This was normal procedure that any law-abiding citizen was expected to follow. The trouble was, he was no longer concerned about the law-abiding part. Even in his disturbed frame of mind he realized that such a wait would be fatal. What he had to know now was *who, if anyone, had been outside.*

Because it seemed of overriding importance to find out if anyone was missing from the dining room, he started to jog back along the path towards the lights of the inn, blocking from his mind his own involvement and possible risk.

He was out of breath as he came to the bar and stopped there while his glance swept the room. He saw at once that the Blake party had gone, but since he had paid that table little attention he knew they could have left before he had started for the bungalow five or ten—how the hell long had it been?—minutes earlier.

The next fact noted and catalogued was that Michael Atherton was on his feet, apparently settling his check with the waiter. Even as Maxwell watched, the other started straight for the entrance without a glance at his mother's table. There Dorothy Atherton was also standing with George Osborne, napkin still in hand as he said something to his daughter. Albert Carswell was leaning over talking to Valerie but before Maxwell could move toward the table he became aware that someone had come up behind him. When he turned he saw the bland sardonic face of Leon Carr.

"They do pretty well here Friday nights, don't they?" he said casually.

Maxwell eyed him narrowly, trying to detect something —a glance, an expression, a reaction—that might give him a clue. When he found nothing at all to help, he said:

"Yeah. Are you stagging it tonight?"

"Sort of playing the field. The young married broads get tired dancing with the same old faces."

"Oh?" Maxwell said. "I hadn't noticed," he added, trying to sound indifferent. "In fact, I thought you just came back."

"From where?"

"I wouldn't know. I do know you weren't here when I came in."

Dorothy Atherton had pushed back her chair by the time Maxwell reached the table and was now explaining that there was no need for everyone to leave. Her handsome face was wooden, her eyes busy with her bag. Her tone was flat and remote and only the words were polite.

Perhaps more than anyone, she knew that the party, aside from the food and drinks, had been a flop in every possible way. Now, apparently feeling she had done all she could, she was saying George Osborne would take her home and he was nodding, his weathered face troubled as he glanced at his daughter.

"Please stay," she said to Maxwell. "It's much too early for Valerie to be coming home on a Friday night. You, too, Wanda, I'm sure Albert will be flattered to see you safely home."

Carswell, who had been standing mute and miserable

and weaving slightly as a result of too many drinks, reacted
to the sound of his name. He gave a small but gallant bow
to the girl.

"Delighted, my dear. If you don't mind riding with an
old man."

The girl smiled at him, and Maxwell understood the
effort it must have taken to keep the hurt from showing.
Never a vivacious girl, she had seemed unusually attractive tonight with her lovely complexion, the sweet mouth,
the sad hazel eyes that had no part in the smile she managed from time to time. Now she touched the older man's
arm affectionately and was kind with her refusal.

"I'd love to, Albert. But you will excuse me tonight,
won't you? I have a dull, annoying headache, probably
because I had too much wine with dinner . . . Would you
mind awfully dropping me off, Father, on your way to the
Hall?"

"Of course he doesn't mind," Dorothy Atherton said.

"If you're sure you wouldn't rather stay," Osborne said.
"As a matter of fact, Dorothy and I would appreciate having you for a chauffeur, at least as far as our place."

Maxwell, who had moved round to Valerie, held her
hand beneath the table. When the others had gone and
Carswell had excused himself and weaved off toward the
bar, they sat down.

The girl gave him a rueful smile and the faintest of
shrugs. "One for the road and we'll go, all right?"

"Perfect," Maxwell said and signaled a waiter. "As a
matter of fact, I'm beat."

"It was pretty awful, wasn't it? I think Mother has a
touch of madness about her to think that anyone here at
the table could possibly have had anything remotely re-
sembling a good time. I think I felt sorriest for Wanda.
Sitting there with her back to the man she's in love with,
not seeing him with that horrible—and I really mean it—

wife of yours but imagining the worst, if that's possible."

Maxwell made some automatic response. Determined to keep his tone easy and offhand, he took care that the things he felt were not reflected in his face. His remarks and the girl's reactions over the next several minutes remained hazy and oddly vague when he tried to recall them the following day.

Luckily, Valerie did most of the talking as though, unable until now because of the others to speak her mind, she had been waiting for the chance to find a sympathetic and understanding listener. This enabled him to keep his genial expression frozen and required no more than an occasional nod. The rest of his mind was occupied with theories and hypothetical conclusions that got him nowhere.

For he understood finally that, to his own knowledge, anyone who had been present could have killed his wife. He had paid little or no attention to what anyone else was doing or when. The time required to go to the bungalow and return was less than five minutes.

As for motives, there were altogether too many.

Sam Blake and Tony Russo were now home free on their long-contemplated purchase of Bastique. Albert Carswell had his well-earned commission in his hip pocket. George Osborne and his daughter—yes, and Dorothy Atherton, too —could continue their determined matchmaking. Leon Carr—

That stopped him, until he remembered both the man's profession and the character of his wife, who had developed the art of willfully aggravating men to a high degree of perfection. Even Michael, if they had quarreled, if she had laughed or taunted or belittled or perhaps destroyed what he had come to think of as love.

And overshadowing such thoughts was the inescapable and overwhelming conclusion that he was becoming more deeply involved with each passing hour by his decision to keep silent. The questions that followed kept repeating themselves and eroding his self-control.

Why hadn't her body already been discovered?

What was his story to be when the police finally came for him?

"Okay, Val," he said, brought back to reality by some movement beside him and relieved to see she was ready to leave. He could not quite hide his embarrassment when he realized he had no idea what she had last said. "I'm sorry."

She made a face at him, but the humorous lights in the green eyes told him he was forgiven.

"I don't mind the sound of my own voice," she said, "but within limits, Alan, within limits. I usually prefer an interested audience, you know? Preferably a live one."

He forced a chuckle which sounded quite authentic. He squeezed her arm as they came out to the parking area. He said tomorrow would be different and that he'd call her in the morning. When he looked back through the trees toward the second bungalow, it seemed quite dark.

9

ALAN MAXWELL NEVER MADE his promised morning call.

The sound that jarred him instantly awake was a determined hammering on his door, and his reactions were varied and somewhat unrelated.

The first was an honest irritation at being so rudely disturbed, but it did make him sit up and swing his feet to the board floor. The hangover that at once made itself felt did nothing to impede the flood of thoughts that had lain dormant. Now they came back with a rush.

It had started to pour right after he'd had his chaste goodnight kiss from Valerie, forcing him to drive at a crawl along the narrow winding roads. He had thought he might have a drink and sit up until the police came, a notion he discarded as making little sense.

He had said, "The hell with it!" and climbed into bed. Apparently he had fallen asleep at once to the timpanic chorus of the heavy shower on the tin roof . . .

"Yeah, yeah, *yeah!*" he called when the knocking was repeated.

The police, it seemed, had finally made it. But did they have to be so damn noisy about it?

He grabbed a pair of shorts to cover his nakedness,

strode barefoot to the door, and flung it open. It was then that he got the first surprise of the day.

For, having prepared himself as well as he could in the few seconds given him to greet the authorities, he could only stare slack-jawed at a very distressed Oscar Jones.

Bewildered as he was in that first moment, he was still able to note that the man's brown face seemed oddly pale and tight, the whites of the dark eyes enormous.

"Come, Mister Max, please."

"Come where? What is it?"

"Trouble. Bad trouble."

"All right, Oscar," Maxwell said, sensing somehow that in his mate's present worked-up condition argument would be useless. "Have I got time for a shave and a cup of coffee?"

Oscar shook his head violently. He was barefoot and clad in an old khaki shirt and trousers, the cuffs rolled up, his everyday working costume. Now he started down the hall with a beckoning gesture.

"No time for that, sir. No time at all."

"Okay, Oscar, okay."

Stepping back inside the room, he pulled a jersey over his head, yanked on a pair of slacks, and found his sneakers. He slammed the door behind him and trotted down the hall, giving his hair a finger comb. As he went down the stairs he tried to guess what it was that might have upset the man so, and then he stopped guessing because he felt a growing inner disturbance that grew alarmingly and made further thought impossible.

He saw as he reached the veranda that Oscar was waiting at the end of the spindly pier out front—an ancient and mostly useless structure, since there was only about three feet of water at the end. Oscar had apparently rowed the dinghy here instead of the accustomed place at the Aquatic Club jetty and he was already at the oars when Maxwell stepped down.

They covered the distance quickly and in silence, Oscar keeping his gaze fixed on the planking and Maxwell understanding it would do no good to probe. He had remained standing and he stepped aboard the ketch as Oscar swung alongside. He waited until the dinghy was made fast and Oscar had joined him before he spoke.

"All right, Oscar. Now what's this all about?"

"Down there," Oscar said and pointed to the open companionway.

"Okay, show me."

"No, sir. You don't need Oscar there. See for yourself."

No longer even daring to speculate but conscious of his growing uneasiness, Maxwell ducked and descended to the main cabin. The light was bad here after the sunshine, but the familiar hum of the generator told him that Oscar had started the tiny engine. He saw the huddled form a moment later at the foot of the sofa berth.

It was the red dress that told him the rest of the story and there was no need for a closer inspection. The only difference was that the body of his wife now lay on its side.

He was never sure how long he stood there, staring sightlessly down, his brain confused and stunned, a sickening emptiness inside him as he tried to grasp the purpose and meaning of Oscar's grim discovery.

It took a tremendous mental effort to concentrate on anything at all and some horrible fascination kept him rooted there until he forced himself to turn away.

Oscar sat with his feet on the stern seat, his buttocks over the coaming on the narrow deck. He had the same scared look in his eyes, the same immobility of features. Maxwell understood that it was not just the shock of death that lingered but the attitude of a man about to be blamed for something he hadn't done.

"Was the cabin door locked when you came aboard, Oscar?"

"No, sir."

"Did you lock up Thursday afternoon?"

"I thought so, but I couldn't rightly swear to it."

"You started the generator."

"First thing. Before I look around."

"Did you touch her?" When he saw the hesitation and some signs of evasiveness he added, "It doesn't matter. I just wondered how you knew she was dead."

"First I call out two, three times. Then I get scared and look at the face. I remember from that other time long ago. I make myself take her hand. Too cold and stiff. I come for you."

Maxwell nodded, knowing what he had to do. "All right. You sit tight. I'll go to the club and phone the police and—"

"No, sir." Oscar shook his head, his tone emphatic. "I don't stay with a dead person."

Maxwell understood that too, for he understood the inbred superstitions so common in the islands.

"Okay, you go. Get police headquarters and ask for Inspector Larkin, understand? Keep at it until you get him. Tell him to come here, and notify Dr. Singh and anyone else needed for a murder investigation. You can wait and row them out."

Oscar needed no urging. He cast off, scrambled into the dinghy, and grabbed the oars. Maxwell watched him go and then sank down on the seat, his hangover thriving and a strange sickness eating at him. It was not just the thought of the coming investigation and the suspicions which were bound to come; it was the unnerving knowledge that the murderer had not been satisfied to kill and take his chances. To plant the body here sometime during the night could be nothing more than a deliberate attempt to frame him, Alan Maxwell.

As he stood trying to make a reasonable assessment of the situation and the motives behind it, some brain cell flicked his thoughts into a new and unwanted channel which demanded attention and forced him to probe his emotional reactions.

He realized then that he felt very little pity or compassion. The knowledge disturbed him deeply—until he understood that the time for such basic emotions had come and gone last night when, as he stood shocked and bewildered in the presence of death, some noise outside the bungalow window had frightened him into thinking only of himself and his own predicament.

Now, making a deliberate and conscious effort to block out all thoughts of the past, he accepted the fact of murder as realistically as he could and tried to consider the most sensible way to face the investigation which would begin all too soon.

He wanted a drink badly and knew he wouldn't take one. He had left without cigarettes. There were some below and after denying the nagging desire for a minute or two he went for them, his eyes avoiding the still figure and trying not to anticipate the trouble which had to follow, had always followed, her.

Presently another impulse came to him and he looked carefully about before he obeyed it. Here in the protected waters the sea was glassy, the immediate stillness broken only by the distant traffic sounds on the highway as the upcountry women went to market. The club was deserted except for a lone black boy going through the motions of sweeping the veranda. At this hour the launch which ferried guests from Young's Island to the club pier had not yet started its daily schedule.

Satisfied, he stripped and dived over the offside of the ketch, surfaced, and rolled onto his back to watch the cloud patches in the blue sky and examine the wispy streamers on the nearest peak.

He felt a lot better, at least physically, when he climbed aboard, and he sat hidden from sight on the cockpit deckboards and let the sun dry him. He was dressed and somehow refreshed fifteen minutes later, when activity started on the club veranda.

There appeared to be five in the official party: two constables in the daytime uniforms, two in plainclothes carrying equipment cases, and the distinctive figure of Inspector Larkin. He did not see Dr. Singh and wondered about it; neither did he see any ambulance attendants. It was apparently decided that two trips would be made in the dinghy, and Larkin and the two plainclothesmen made up the first boatload.

Maxwell gave them a hand as they came aboard. Larkin nodded formally but seemed in no hurry to start the inquiry. He was a handsome ebony-skinned man with close-cut hair, regular features and intelligent maroon-colored eyes. Although he sometimes wore plainclothes, he was usually in uniform, as he was now, the khaki jacket with half-sleeves and polished brown belt and the matching shorts looking as if they had just come off the ironing board. The tan knee-length socks showed no wrinkle and his tan oxfords had a hard shine; the uniform cap was centered. A swagger stick under one arm completed the picture, and when Maxwell became aware that he was not the object of the man's fixed glance, he turned to follow it just in time to see the government launch clear the small headland by the Villa Inn, the size of the white bow-wave suggesting a throttle well open.

"Your man said there was a body aboard," Larkin said by way of explanation. "It will be easier to remove it by sea instead of ferrying it ashore by dinghy. The ambulance can wait at the government dock. There *is* a body?" he added with a glance at the open companionway.

"Below. It's my wife. Oscar discovered her when he came aboard and then got me out of bed."

"I see." Larkin hesitated, his expression grave. He had a precise and rather formal way of speaking that might be thought stilted by an American used to the diction of the times. Now, his reluctance showing, he said: "Your wife? I'm sorry, Mr. Maxwell. I'm afraid this is going to be rather difficult. I heard she was visiting the colony."

He paused again, frowning, but relieved somehow that the amenities were over. "This door"—he pointed the stick —"was open?"

"It's usually locked at night, but Oscar wasn't sure."

"Did you touch your wife when you came, move her in any way?"

Maxwell started to say no; then caught himself, as he realized that such a reply would be unrealistic under the circumstances. You found a woman crumpled on the cabin floor, you made some effort to find out why.

"Just her hand. It was already cold and sort of stiff."

"Shall we have a look while we're waiting for the doctor?" He spoke to the two plainclothesmen, one apparently the photographer and the other the fingerprint man: "Give me a minute and then you can get at it."

He turned to Maxwell, who shook his head. "If you don't mind, I'd rather stay here."

Larkin gave him a quick, understanding look and nodded. "Quite. Must have been frightfully shocking, finding her like that. You had no idea she'd been aboard at any time?"

Maxwell said no, and Larkin, noticing the dinghy come alongside with the two constables, ordered them back to the pier.

"See that no one comes out here without my permission. Try to keep the dock clear."

Now Oscar Jones spoke up: "Will you want me, Inspector?"

Larkin thought it over. "Not for the time being." And Maxwell said, "Why don't you stay ashore until I need you?"

Larkin turned and went quickly below. Maxwell sat down, momentarily relieved, but understanding that he

had to be ready for the questions that were bound to follow. Larkin was back in what seemed less than a minute.
When he had motioned the two technicians below he sat
down beside Maxwell to watch the approaching police
launch.

"You are quite right," he said. "Dead for some time, it
would appear. Do you know how she died?"

"No."

"A small-caliber bullet. Unless the doctor finds some
other sign of violence."

He was silent then, and Maxwell stood up to put out
fenders as the police launch slowed its approach and the
engine idled. It was well done, with just a quick thrust of
reverse as one of the hands came nimbly aboard with a line
while the other fended off the starboard bow and tossed
another line to Maxwell.

Dr. Boy Singh, who had been leaning against the cabin,
clinging to a grabrail, stepped aboard, a neat, trim-figured
man in a dark business suit. His smooth skin had a yellow-
ish-tan cast, his hair was jet black and straight, and wide-
rimmed glasses magnified slightly his soft brown eyes.

He had been educated in Port of Spain and at McGill
Medical and had come to the colony four or five years
earlier. Maxwell was not familiar in a professional sense
with the island's two other doctors, but the way Singh had
treated a nasty gash on the heel of his thumb some months
before convinced him that should he need medical treat-
ment in the future, Singh would be the man. In addition
to his private practice, he was the police physician and
medical examiner, handling what pathology there was at
the hospital.

Now he nodded politely to Maxwell, said good morning
to Larkin. Light flashes were already popping from the
companionway as the photographer did his work, and
when Larkin had filled the doctor in, Singh said:

"I imagine it's a bit cramped down there. I'll wait till your men finish, I think."

"A few more minutes won't make much difference," Larkin said. "I feel sure the body has been there for some time."

He called down to the cabin, glanced at his watch, tucked his stick back under his arm as his impatience began to show. When the photographer appeared with his bulky case the Inspector nodded to Singh.

"All right, Doctor. It's all yours. My fingerprint man will keep out of your way. It's probably a useless gesture in any case."

Singh was not gone long before he reappeared. He did not come topside but called up through the opening.

"You are quite right, Inspector. Death occurred many hours ago. As a guess, I'd say probabl / between nine and midnight, give or take a bit. A small-caliber bullet that may have glanced from a bone and nicked the heart. I will have it for you when I do the post-mortem."

He paused as though uncertain how to continue. Maxwell had the feeling he kept his glance purposely averted, and when Singh spoke again knew why.

"Before we remove her I would like to do one more thing. It will be necessary to partly unclothe the body. As her husband, would you care to assist me, Mr. Maxwell?"

Maxwell recoiled inwardly at the thought. He let his breath out and shook his head. "I'd prefer not to, Doctor."

Singh nodded sympathetically. "I quite understand. Well—"

He let the thought dangle and disappeared. When he came up perhaps three or four minutes later he was ready to go ashore.

"The somewhat awkward position of the body," he said, "made me think death might have occurred elsewhere. Post-mortem lividity confirmed my suspicions."

"Post-mortem lividity?" Maxwell said.

"When a person dies the heart stops and circulation ceases. Gravity drains the blood to the low points of the body wherever they may be. A definite discoloration takes place and once coagulation starts, these darker spots remain. Should the body be moved soon after death occurs, such lividity is less pronounced. This was not true in your wife's case. The buttocks and shoulder blades indicate that she died on her back and was not moved until at least an hour or more after that."

He signaled to the launch and two white-coated assistants came across with a rolled-up stretcher, straps, and a blanket. Larkin thanked Singh and, taking Maxwell by the arm, turned him toward the bow.

"We can talk better up there."

When they were by themselves he added, "I'm going to have to ask you a great many questions, I'm afraid. For the most part this would be more convenient in my office, where a recorder is available so that your statement can be transcribed. But I should warn you now that anything you say may be used against you in a court of law.

"For the present, however, I will confine myself to the immediate background. When you last saw her, who else might have seen her or been with her—things like that, so that when I leave I can radio headquarters and have a man question such persons. Now when did you see your wife last?"

"She was renting a bungalow at the Villa Inn."

"So I understand."

"I talked to her late Thursday afternoon in the bungalow. A guy from Boston, Massachusetts, named Leon Carr was present."

"I know about him."

"The last time I saw her was last night, at the weekly buffet dinner."

"You weren't with her?"

"Michael Atherton was. They had a table for two."

"You were alone, then?"

Maxwell said no, and went on to relate the essentials about Dorothy Atherton's group. He was necessarily vague about individual movements, because he had paid no particular attention to the various goings and comings. He did give a rough idea of who left with whom and the approximate time.

Larkin had been tapping his stick against his muscular calf as he accepted this information.

"Very well," he said. "You may find you can be more specific in my office—but for now, one more question. Have you any idea why anyone should take the risk of moving the body here, no doubt in the middle of the night?"

"No!"

"No enemies?"

"Not that kind of enemies. I can think of some motives, others who might like my wife dead. Unless someone wanted to frame me, knowing I certainly had a motive, the only reason I can think of would be to delay the discovery of the body for some reason. Either that, or with the idea of lousing up your investigation."

Because he wanted more than anything to get off the *Annabel* as quickly as possible he said:

"Look, Inspector. Is it all right if I come in by myself? I'd like a shave and some breakfast and a change of clothes—"

"Quite all right. I'll expect you in an hour."

10

THE DOOR OF THE Police Commissioner's office at the front
of the headquarters building stood open, but the room beyond was empty and Alan Maxwell remembered that that
official was on leave. Across the hall was the somewhat
smaller office of the acting commissioner and Chief Super-
intendent. Adjacent to it at the rear Larkin, as the head of
CID, had a small anteroom, and Maxwell knocked at the
closed door beyond.

This was opened by a tall Negro in plainclothes wearing
a tan suit with a white shirt. His skin was lighter than
Larkin's, a sort of café-au-lait shade; but his features were
coarser and his broad face was long in the jaw and, at the
moment, expressionless.

Larkin introduced him as Sergeant Beaman. "The sergeant is going out to search your wife's bungalow and item-
ize her possessions. There is also a good chance that she was
killed there. We intend to find out. You have no objections?"

"None."

Larkin's nod dismissed the sergeant, and he waved Maxwell to a chair and indicated the tape recorder.

"If you are ready I will begin by asking you to identify
yourself and repeating the warning I gave you earlier."

"Okay," Maxwell said dryly. "But if this can be used against me there are a lot of things I'm going to have to skip."

"Such as?"

"Opinions, guesses, things like that. I'm not going to put anyone on the spot, not on tape."

Larkin leaned back, head tipping slightly, his eyes half-closed as he considered the remark. He rubbed a thumb absently along the hinge of his jaw. After five seconds of this he let the spring in his chair bring him forward and slid his forearms across the desktop, his dark gaze focusing and full of thought.

"Very well." He pushed the recorder aside. "Your idea has merit. At this point your informal opinions and thoughts may have more value than a statement which can be taken later. Suppose you start by telling me something about your wife as you knew her. How long have you been separated?"

"Nearly two years."

"You left, or did she—"

"I left."

"Why?"

"She was too much for me."

"Before I ask you in what way, suppose you describe her in your own words. Not physically. I've seen her. A very attractive woman. Wealthy too, I understand. How wealthy? A million—"

"That's what I thought when we were married. I mean, I figured she might have an income of forty or fifty thousand a year. It was more like ten times that."

"And that became a problem for you?"

"Not in itself." Maxwell slouched in his native-built chair and stretched his legs, his tanned face somber and the dark eyes brooding as he tried to concentrate but still not sure how far he should go. "Describe her in my own words?" he asked finally. "Like with adjectives?"

"Why not try some? I'll keep in mind that you may be prejudiced."

"Well, I'd say she was, among other things, aggressive, selfish, possessive, intemperate, domineering, unpredictable; she could be vicious, vindictive, vituperative; she seemed dedicated somehow to the destruction of a man's ego and self-respect."

"And on the plus side?"

The unexpected question demanded attention, and Maxwell was surprised to find he could grin.

"She was deceptively compliant when she wanted to be. She was smart, intelligent, generous when it pleased her. She was also marvelous in bed when she was in the mood, which was frequent. She was a chameleon, Inspector. Greatly appealing one day and coldly vindictive the next.

"Ask George Osborne or Michael Atherton," he went on, warming to his subject. "Osborne says she had Michael eating out of her hand in five days. Yesterday there was a big meeting at the Hall—I can tell you about it if you like—and Michael made clear, or she did and he didn't correct her, that they were going to be married when she got her divorce. Believe me, she was a master—or should it be mistress?—of enticement."

"Hmm." Larkin nodded again, still thoughtful. "And you were married how long?"

"Just about nine months."

"You left abruptly? Why?"

"I'd had all I could take," Maxwell said, and went on to repeat most of the things he had told Valerie Atherton when he had met her plane. For a moment only, he considered speaking of the shots Louise had fired, and his panic-stricken scramble for his life; then decided against it. He did explain about the layoff at his office and the timely cable from Osborne offering the *Annabel* for sale.

"Did you wonder why she did not divorce you?"

"From time to time. She could have whenever she'd wanted to."

"Have you any idea why she should come here at this time?"

"Sure I've got an idea," Maxwell said, his annoyance showing now as he recalled what Louise had done to him. "I think she just couldn't bear the thought of me, or any man, walking out on her. I think the idea kept bugging her until she couldn't stand it any longer."

He shifted his weight, scowled at nothing in particular, and told Larkin about the two husbands who had preceded him and what had happened to them.

"From what I've heard about Leon Carr, I'd say she hired him to locate me. He did. He's been hanging around three weeks, plenty of time to find out all there is to know about me. She came down to make as much trouble for me as she could, and she had five or six days to think about it while I was away."

"So I understand. You're referring to your boat?"

Maxwell turned the scowl on the Inspector's impassive face. "You know about that?"

Larkin tipped one hand, the dark eyes mildly amused. "We have men in plainclothes. They have contacts. They have learned how to listen as well as ask questions. Then we sift the facts from the rumors. I have heard that Mr. Osborne sold his interest in your ketch to your wife."

"You heard right," Maxwell said, his voice tight. "If you want to know what else she was trying to do to run me off the island, I'll tell you . . . You know Bastique is to be sold?"

Larkin nodded. "To a company called Island Development, I believe. This would have something to do with the meeting at Hardin Hall you referred to earlier?"

Maxwell said yes, and then he was talking in quick hard phrases. All the pressure, harassment, and resentment that had been building up inside him came out with a vehemence that surprised him as he spoke of his wife's offer and his own involvement as the company architect.

Only when he had run out of breath and his anger had begun to dissipate did he realize that everything he had said, when added up and analyzed, presented a lovely motive for murder. The sudden shrill of the telephone came as a welcome respite.

Larkin said, "Excuse me," and then: "Yes? . . . Yes, Doctor . . . One moment and I'll ask him." He palmed the handset. "Do you know if it was customary for your wife to wear a ring on the third finger of the left hand?"

Maxwell, recalling when he had last seen it, said yes.

"Did you see this ring recently?"

"She was wearing it when I went to see her Thursday afternoon."

"Yes, Doctor," Larkin spoke again into the handset. "Yes. Very good, and thanks for calling." To Maxwell he added, "Singh noticed ring marks on that hand but no ring. He wondered about it."

He opened a desk drawer and put a ring and a wristwatch Maxwell had seen before on the desk. The ring was a sapphire-and-diamond cocktail piece; the platinum watch was diamond-studded, its band paved with small stones.

"I thought it might be prudent to remove them from the body." Larkin replaced the pieces and leaned back, clasping his hands behind his neck. His dark gaze slid away for a thoughtful moment and he brought it back. "Third finger of the left hand? Would that have some special significance?"

Maxwell grunted, impressed again by the Inspector's astuteness. "It was her engagement ring, which she paid for," he said, his tone sardonic, "and I put on her finger. An emerald with diamond baguettes. Twenty-two thousand bucks, American."

The announcement brought a look of surprise, the first Larkin had shown. He whistled silently, but before he could speak the telephone rang once more.

Again he excused himself. "Larkin . . . Yes, Sergeant."

There was a long silence while his glance strayed idly about the room. "Well, keep it." He glanced at his watch. "I'll be along shortly. And one other thing. There seems to be a ring missing," he said, and went on to describe it.

He hung up and let his chair come forward once more. "Would you know the name and address of your wife's attorneys?"

Maxwell named the firm. "On Congress Street," he said, "but I don't know the number."

"Do you know if there are any close relatives?"

"I never heard her mention any."

"Would you know the terms of her will?"

"No."

"I'll get in touch with someone there. Do you think the office would be open on Saturday?"

"Someone should be there, or at least an answering service."

"Apparently you are still the legal husband but just what your rights are, I wouldn't know. No doubt the lawyers will want to fly someone down to make funeral arrangements and claim the body unless you—"

"No."

"Umm . . . Yes . . . Well, your consul will be notified, and perhaps the ambassador in Barbados . . . Now about the Bastique business," he said in swift digression. "I know about your Mr. Blake, of course."

He paused to take up a typed sheet, apparently a copy from immigration. "Traveling with a Mr. Russo and two women." His brows arched. "Wives, would you say?"

"Companions," Maxwell said, a small grin showing. "Maybe secretaries."

"Yes," Larkin said. "And attractive, no doubt . . . Now, since you've been working for this development company you probably investigated them to some extent. So did we, naturally. They seem to be a substantial organization and quite legitimate. Is that your impression?"

Maxwell said yes, and repeated the rumor given him of the possibility there might be some Syndicate or Mafia money somewhere in the background.

"But if there is," he added, "I don't see how it concerns me."

"But if your company were to lose out because of some offer made by your wife—"

For the third time the telephone interrupted him and this time his annoyance showed as he answered. It did not last, however, and he said:

"Give me three minutes and then send him in."

He stood up and moved to the window, his back to the room and his hands clasped behind him. After a minute, he turned and leaned stiff-armed on the desk.

"Michael Atherton," he said. "Captain Andrews, my chief assistant, will be talking to Mr. Osborne and Mr. Carswell and possibly to Mrs. Atherton. What I am about to do may be somewhat unorthodox, but at this point it might be helpful to have you remain. Unless, of course, Mr. Atherton objects."

He remained standing until the door opened and Atherton entered the room, spotted Maxwell, hesitated, and then closed the door carefully behind him.

"Good morning," Larkin said. "I appreciate your coming. Please sit down."

Maxwell noted the change in Atherton, and because he understood that the latter's infatuation for the dead woman had been real and all-consuming, he could appreciate how shocking the news of her murder must have been. Unless—

He blocked out that thought and assessed the signs of strain and the lack of color in the handsome features. The blue eyes had a dull, resigned look; but there was some wariness too as he sat down and faced Larkin.

"My call this morning was the first knowledge you had about what happened to Mrs. Maxwell? . . . I'm sorry it had to be that way," Larkin said when Atherton nodded, "but it is essential that we get on with our investigation as quickly as possible. Frankly, at this stage, we have very little to go on."

He went on to repeat some of the things Maxwell had told him; then added, "Although I must warn you that anything you say may be used against you in a court of law, I should point out that this interview—and it shouldn't take long—is informal and will not be taken down. On the other hand, you have the right at any time to refuse to answer any or all questions.

"Now, according to Mr. Maxwell, he last saw you sometime around ten last evening, on your feet talking to your waiter. He thought you might be settling your bill."

"I probably was."

"Mrs. Maxwell had left some time before that?"

"Yes."

"How long would you say?"

"Twenty minutes, a half hour."

"You decided she was not coming back? You had said good night?"

"There were no good nights."

"Oh? You quarreled?"

"We did." Atherton's mouth tightened briefly and his blue eyes were remote and smouldering. "At least she did."

"Mr. Maxwell has told me about the meeting at the Hall yesterday afternoon. It was his impression that you had planned to marry Mrs. Maxwell once she had her freedom."

Atherton gave Maxwell a scathing glance, but he answered truthfully. "That's what I thought . . . Look, Inspector," he said flatly as signs of ill temper began to show. "You've heard of lovers' quarrels? So what's so unusual about this one?"

"Could you tell me what led to yours?" Larkin asked patiently.

"I had been thinking how upset my mother and sister were when they found out about Louise's determination to buy Bastique. I happened to mention I didn't think it was that important, that perhaps she'd reconsider. She disagreed. One word led to another."

He paused then, his distress showing. "It seemed to me she didn't care a damn about owning the island, that she was only buying it to spite Alan . . . I'd never seen her like that before. I mean, all of a sudden she was furious with me. I'd never heard her talk that way. When I tried to reason with her—I couldn't very well apologize for simply making a harmless suggestion—she wouldn't listen. She said she'd buy the damn island whether I liked it or not. Before I realized it, she'd grabbed her bag and was gone."

He let his breath come out and his chin sagged, his gaze unfocused and downcast. Larkin let the silence build for ten seconds before he said:

"You didn't follow her to the bungalow? You knew where it was. You'd been there before?"

"Of course I had. Several times." With that he pushed his chair back and stood up. "I'm afraid there's nothing more I can tell you, Inspector," he said, his voice polite but determined. "I'll admit when I walked out last night I was pretty damn angry, but I didn't follow her and I didn't kill her; I don't know who did or why."

He gave Larkin a quick nod of dismissal, repeated the gesture to Maxwell; then he was gone.

Larkin's eyes remained on the closed door for some seconds; then he shrugged absently and reached for the telephone.

"I'm going over to the Villa Inn for a few minutes. If Captain Andrews returns before I do, ask him to wait. I shouldn't be too long." To Maxwell he added, "Let's take a ride," and picked up his cap and swagger stick.

11

Because he had his own car and had been told he need not return to Police Headquarters, Alan Maxwell followed the police sedan to the Villa Inn and parked beside it. Nothing was said as he automatically followed Larkin's erect and impressive figure down the curving path to the second bungalow.

Sergeant Beaman straightened as the door opened, but the fingerprint man, the same one who had been aboard the *Annabel,* continued working with his powders, camel's hair brushes, and print-lifting paraphernalia. Maxwell stopped just inside the door and glanced about the room, cataloguing the now-familiar furnishings but deliberately avoiding the spot where he had found his wife the night before. He was vaguely aware that the Sergeant had given something to Larkin, and presently the Inspector beckoned.

He was holding one hand palm up, and Maxwell saw then that he held two empty small-caliber shells.

".25's," he said. "American make. Of course, the automatic could have been manufactured anywhere these days, but the fact they are American, as was your wife—" He broke off and tried another tangent: "From your knowledge, was she the sort of woman who might travel with a small gun?"

"Yes."

"You know this to be a fact?"

"You said *might*. She had a little Colt .25 when I was married to her. She didn't go around carrying it but we traveled some, and I can remember two occasions when she had it . . . Did they find the other slug?" he asked, wanting to get off the subject.

"Not yet, but they will. Sergeant Beaman has been busy taking an inventory of her personal effects . . . By the way, he questioned both the owner and the head barman, Francis, and they corroborated your statement although, like you, they cannot pinpoint exact times or movements. They recall that your wife left young Atherton at the table, that he left alone. They also state that the Blake party left early. I'll get to them later in the day."

For a moment he seemed to have lost his original train of thought; but it soon came back. "Oh, yes, the bullets. Corporal Howard will be on the lookout for the missing one as he goes about his work, and the sergeant will give him a hand . . . Every inch, Sergeant," he added. "Pillows, mattresses, furniture. The walls too, in case there is a scar where a bullet might have fragmented.

"One thing," he said, pointing. "The window and door are intact, and if it went through there"—he pointed now at the long high window in the other wall—"the angle, if an ordinary person held the gun, would be all but impossible. Now what do we have, Sergeant?"

He had been moving as he spoke and now stopped at the coffee table, on which stood three pocketbooks or handbags and their contents—a mound of jewelry, lipsticks, compacts, tissues, currency both American and local, some sheets of paper.

"You have inventoried this as you went along?"

"Yes, sir," Beaman said. "This is about all of it."

"What about an emerald and diamond ring?" Larkin began to separate the individual pieces with the tip of his stick.

"Not here, sir. At least not yet."

"Spread them out, item by item. Perhaps Mr. Maxwell can help us." He examined the currency as he spoke, separating the Biwi dollars from the American. "No traveler's checks?"

"No, sir."

"Would she be carrying such checks?" Larkin turned to Maxwell. "I mean, on a trip such as this?"

"Probably. Although I know she had established credit at Barclay's for at least four hundred thousand."

"U.S.?" Larkin said, his surprise showing. "Well—"

It was clear that he was unaccustomed to thinking in such terms, and he tried again when he had counted the bills once more.

"Two twenty-dollar bills, your money. Fifteen and change, Biwi. Was there any checkbook, Sergeant?"

"Not that I recall, sir."

"Then I'd say she had traveler's checks," Maxwell said. "She wouldn't be traveling that light."

Larkin squared the bills neatly and replaced the stack. "Now what about these?" he said, and began to separate the jewelry.

Some of it was gold—a heavy link bracelet and two pins that had foreign-looking designs. There was an old-fashioned brooch of turquoise and silver that was either a souvenir or something of sentimental value; two sets of earrings, one gold and one platinum with tiny diamonds rimming larger, pear-shaped stones.

As he considered the assortment it seemed to Maxwell that something was missing, a favorite piece of some kind, distinctive enough to set it apart. He kept probing, trying to jog his memory. Finally, about to give up, he recalled what it was but just then Larkin was talking.

"I expect she had more at home," he said, frowning absently.

"She did. A diamond-and-platinum bracelet that must have cost a fortune, I don't know how many pairs of earrings. But there was one pin, a favorite of hers, I don't see here."

"And you think it should be?"

"She always took it on our trips. She was wearing it the first time we met."

"Describe it, please."

"It was a simple design but distinctive. A circle maybe an inch and a half in diameter, with a little tail that reminded me of a capital Q. Platinum, paved with square-cut diamonds maybe a quarter or three-sixteenths of an inch each."

"Then, if you are right, there are two pieces missing— that pin and the emerald ring, both very valuable. Well, that gives us something definite to look for, doesn't it?" Then, with no change of inflection, he said, "Would you mind turning out your pockets?"

Maxwell eyed him crookedly and obeyed. He patted himself to demonstrate that there was nothing more. When Larkin nodded to indicate he was to replace his things, Maxwell said:

"Sure you don't want to search my room too?"

"That is being done. Just routine, of course."

"Sort of a sneaky way of doing things, isn't it, Inspector?"

"In my business"—the tone remained quiet and unruffled —"I deal with a lot of sneaky people . . . Could I have your inventory, Sergeant?"

Beaman brought over his clipboard, and Maxwell saw the hand-printed list the Sergeant had made.

"Check that, please, with what you see here," Larkin said to Maxwell. "If it tallies with your count, sign it."

When Maxwell had done so, he saw that Larkin was holding some letter-size papers. From where he stood he thought one was a legal form of some kind, and he guessed its contents before Larkin identified it.

"This has to do with your ketch," he said. "If she had lived I gather that she could have dispossessed you."

"Not necessarily," Maxwell argued, and repeated what George Osborne had told him. "She conned George into thinking she was going to make me a present of my debt, but luckily he did not cash the check. When he found out what she was really like and what she was doing to Michael Atherton, he hung onto the check. He still has it."

He spread his hands, dark eyes challenging. "In any case it's academic, isn't it? With my wife dead, that check cannot be cashed. I have an idea the executors would rather have that nine thousand back than a lien on a boat they wouldn't know what to do with if they had it."

He thought he saw a small gleam of respect in Larkin's thoughtful appraisal, and watched his small nod.

"You have a point," he said, "but the fact remains that your wife's sudden death at this time was most convenient. I mean, for you."

"And for a few others, if you want to put it that way."

"In any event, I shall impound all her effects." He waved his stick in an all-inclusive gesture. "These"—he tapped the papers—"I'll keep separate pending the arrival of your wife's executors . . . Anything yet, Sergeant?" he added, turning to Beaman and the fingerprint man, who were still examining the room and its contents.

"Not yet, sir."

"Keep at it. Every inch. I must get back."

This announcement brought a welcome sense of relief for Maxwell, who had already had more than enough of Larkin and his questions. He found a cigarette and got it going, hoping he sounded casual and indifferent when he said:

"Will that be all for now, Inspector?"

"You will keep yourself available?"

"Certainly."

"I appreciate your cooperation," Larkin said; and then, with some new edge in his voice: "However, I must remind you that I still need a formal signed statement. Perhaps I should also warn you that as of now you remain the principal suspect in this affair. A husband usually is."

"So I've been told," Maxwell said flatly, dark eyes steady. "And thanks for the warning."

"In your case," Larkin said, ignoring the comment, "we have a broken marriage, a wife who hires a private investigator and comes this distance to—you yourself suggested this—do all she can to make trouble for you and destroy your livelihood. It adds up to a classic motive, Mr. Maxwell, at least as good as others you have mentioned, just as you had the same opportunity and lack of alibi."

Maxwell found he did not resent the implication. Instead he consoled himself with the thought of how much worse his position might be, how much stronger the suspicion, if Larkin knew the truth about what had really happened to him in this room last night. He still was not sure he had done the right thing; he only knew that he had told his story and he was stuck with it. Even so, he could not resist one last sardonic remark:

"I suppose having murdered my wife here last night, I then came back later, risking exposure, to move her to my boat so that Oscar Jones would find her."

Larkin allowed himself a small smile, his perfect teeth showing. "Killers do odd things, Mr. Maxwell. In this case it may become a matter of interpretation."

Maxwell got as far as the parking lot before he changed his mind about going back to the *Annabel*. He wanted a drink although his hangover, as such, no longer demanded it. He also had to get lunch sometime. Unable to make up his mind and annoyed by his indecision, he went back inside the inn and slid onto a bar stool.

A few guests were at poolside but there was no sign of Sam Blake's party. He wondered when Larkin was going to question them, or whether Captain Andrews would be detailed for that job. It seemed essential that he, too, see Blake sometime but that could wait a while until he was in a better frame of mind. He considered calling Valerie, but that too could wait until he could think of just what to say, so he sat there brooding, sipping the sugarcane brandy and soda Francis had put before him.

For a few minutes he considered getting some lunch here but he could think of several reasons why this might become awkward. He wondered what the Casurina Inn might offer for lunch and then had a better idea. There were things on board the *Annabel* that could serve, and this supported his desire to be alone for a while until he could sort things out and do some uninterrupted thinking.

12

His room at the inn when he got back around one o'clock was hot and airless, and he stripped and put on the slacks, jersey, and sneakers he had worn earlier. Downstairs he left word that he would be on the *Annabel* and then he picked his way along the narrow stretch of dark-gray, rock-studded sand that was a beach in name only.

The dinghy was there, which told him that Oscar was home and would most certainly stay there now until summoned. He got the oars from underneath the Aquatic Club veranda and pushed off. The channel surface was still, and as he rowed he watched the Young's Island launch swing out from the jetty on the far side.

When he had tied up he saw that the companionway door stood open. This annoyed him until he remembered that he had left with the police technicians still aboard, and realized he could not blame them. He was, he knew, still jumpy and restless, and as he glanced about he could see the black —and sometimes white—smudges where the fingerprint man had worked with his powders.

The generator motor had cut out and it was quiet here, the gentle lap-lap of the wavelets unnoticed unless one listened for them. An inspection of the icebox showed him four eggs, some scraps of ham, bacon, fruit, a half bottle of milk. There were some biscuits in a can and enough bread in the little breadbox for his purpose, stale but not yet moldy.

Having made the momentous decision to whip up a ham omelette, he was now ready for a leisurely drink made to his specifications. His drink cupboard was sizable, since when on charter it had, at all times, to be well stocked. It would need to be replenished if and when he was allowed to take out the scheduled charter, and he saw now that the sugarcane brandy bottle was half full. There was nearly a fifth of Gordon's gin, a still-sealed bottle of Cockade rum, and a half-bottle of Scotch.

At the Casurina his liquor cabinet was at all times locked; here such measures were unnecessary, since Oscar Jones did not drink, limiting himself to an occasional bottle of beer, and then only when asked. Now he got a highball glass and some ice, squeezed a little juice from a fresh slice of lime. He poured the brandy, uncapped a split of soda, and stood at the sink counter to pour. He took that moment to glance out the rectangular port, and before he realized it, the glass was full to overflowing.

Because he was basically an orderly man and did not want to spill on the carpet, he leaned over to suck a bit of the drink before he lifted the glass.

It was this small half-conscious gesture, this built-in respect for neatness, that saved his life.

That first stooped-over sip was less than a mouthful and he had swallowed but a part of this when the bitterness filled his mouth and assaulted his taste buds.

He spat instantly, a reflex response, then spat again. Bewildered and too startled to think, he leaned over, ran the tap, and sucked water from his palm to cleanse his mouth until the taste was gone.

For many seconds then he stared with unseeing dark eyes at the rectangle of light above the sink where the port had been cut in the cabin trunk. Gradually the shock passed, to be replaced by suspicion. Finally, his mind working at last, he was aware of an odd, debilitating fear.

His movements deliberate and calculating now, he put the glass aside and found a teaspoon. He poured a bit of brandy from the bottle, touched it with a little finger and tasted again as carefully as he could. When he was sure of the bitterness he sealed the bottle with trembling fingers.

Again he rinsed out his mouth and thought hard to overcome his jumpy nerves and the tight hard knot in his stomach. He put the sealed Cockade bottle aside and repeated the teaspoon-tasting with the gin and Scotch. Not quite sure with his first test, he tried a slightly more generous sample. Satisfied that these had not been tampered with, he understood finally why the sugarcane brandy had been selected.

It was, in a sense, a private stock, one not offered to charter parties. To the uneducated it was merely rum, which it was in a way. The chief difference lay in the fact that the distillers aged it a few years longer than the ordinary brand of Barbados rum, and when he had a few bottles he kept them out of sight, seldom offering any to guests, an apparent oversight which bothered no one since the locals for the most part preferred whisky.

Yet whoever had used the poison had done so knowing that the odds on anyone but Alan Maxwell drinking from that bottle were prohibitive. Unfortunately, this habit of his was well known to a great many people.

Such thinking settled his nerves, and his initial frightened reaction gave way to an uneasy sickness that came not from his almost miraculous escape from death, but from the very fact that someone familiar with his habits wanted him dead.

The resentment inside still smouldered, but mixed with it now was a determination heretofore missing. Until then he had been able to accept the idea that he had been a victim of circumstances. That someone, most certainly the killer, had made a clumsy and ineffectual effort to frame him by bringing his wife's body aboard could have been prompted by many considerations not necessarily personal.

This was something else, and for the first time he knew that until he had done everything he could to expose the one responsible he could never be satisfied.

This simple resolve helped to restore his self-control, and he reacted by throwing the poisoned highball violently into the sink. When he had rinsed the glass he got more ice and poured generously from the Scotch bottle, adding the soda that remained in the split. He could feel the sudden warmth working on his stomach after the first large swallow. This in turn began at once to lift his spirits and suggest the next move.

From behind a cabinet he took a brown paper bag he had tucked there. It was large enough for the brandy bottle with some to spare, and when he had twisted the excess paper round the neck he put the bottle back in a drawer.

He thought again of his omelette and decided it could wait. Instead he dropped down on the edge of the berth, took another large pull on the Scotch, and flopped back, one bent arm cradling the back of his head. He had no intention of dozing and did not realize he had, until he heard the hail from somewhere nearby.

What had seemed part of a dream became at once a reality when it was repeated, and he swung his legs over the edge and bounded up the first two steps of the ladder. With the sliding hatch back he could see the approaching skiff with George Osborne at the oars and Albert Carswell perched on the stern seat. Carswell, seeing he had gained an audience, repeated the customary greeting, his good humor at once apparent.

"Ahoy the *Annabel!* Request permission to come aboard."

"Permission granted," Maxwell said, and laughed in spite of himself.

He gave Carswell a hand as he clambered aboard while Osborne secured the skiff and followed more deliberately, limping once before he steadied himself and muttering, "Damned arthritis!"

"We phoned the Casurina," Carswell said, with the pleased and self-satisfied air of a man who has just completed a difficult and hazardous mission. That his white drill suit, vest, and felt hat might seem incongruous afloat seemed not to concern him, and his slack, peanut-colored skin looked more alive somehow. "They said you'd be here, so we thought—"

He let the thought, whatever it was, die there. Making one more attempt to explain the reason for this unexpected visit, he began obliquely.

"We were talking at the club over lunch, George and I. You see we both had been visited by Captain Andrews of the CID and . . . Well, I must say it was shocking news, most shocking. And now that we've come I'm not at all sure we should have. I'm afraid I still don't know quite what to say."

Maxwell understood the confusion, just as he understood that there had been three quick rum swizzles before a meager lunch, more than sufficient to give the older man the confidence and initiative so often lacking to satisfy his curiosity.

He opened his mouth to make a conventional reply when some fortunate thrust of instinct warned him to be careful. The thought that he might, right then, have given himself away jarred him, and he cautioned himself to speak with care. For only he knew that he had found his wife, still warm, last night in the bungalow. And that was the way it had to stay—at least for now.

"Sure, Albert," he said, hoping his momentary confusion did not show. "I wouldn't know what to say either. As a matter of fact, I still don't know how I feel. We were strangers, Louise and I, and our dislike was mutual. How would you feel if some bastard killed your wife and then dumped her body in your living room?"

"Quite. We were told the circumstances, and I must say—"

Osborne, always direct, and more so lately because of his heart condition and arthritis, growled an interruption.

"Stop babbling, Albert, damn it! Forget the amenities, can't you? . . . We came because we decided each of us wanted to clarify something and it seemed sensible to come together. *I* want to know how we stand on the *Annabel*, and Albert wants to know if you've heard from this fellow Blake about Bastique."

"Precisely," Carswell said, sounding relieved to have someone else carry the conversation ball. He fluttered his bony hands and managed to indicate the main cabin. "Perhaps a small libation, say a spot of sugarcane brandy or—"

He stopped in mid-sentence, as though warned by the quick hard stare Maxwell could not control. It was a purely involuntary reaction that he regretted, and by then Carswell's expression was bland and the washed-out blue eyes seemed innocent enough. Osborne continued to look truculent and impatient, and Maxwell spoke quickly to cover up.

"All out of brandy, Albert," he said. "I didn't know you cared for it."

"Not a question of caring." Carswell, showing no embarrassment, shrugged expressively. "More a question of affording it, I should think. Then perhaps a drop of whisky."

Maxwell waved them below, still wondering if the reference had some significance or whether he was just getting jumpy as his suspicions got out of hand.

With his guests perched on the edge of one bunk he made Carswell his whisky-and-soda. Gesturing with a smaller glass and seeing Osborne's nod of confirmation, he made a pink gin and spiked his own drink.

"Inspector Larkin knew about your deal with my wife on the *Annabel*," he said addressing Osborne and deciding to get on with their business. "I was with him while the police were searching her room. He showed me the papers and I

told him about the uncashed check. It's no good now anyway, you know."

"So I understand," Osborne said, "not that it makes a
damn bit of difference . . . So what do you think?"

"I think we ought to go along as if nothing had happened,
at least until we get some definite word from the executors
of her estate. I'll make my regular—make that overdue—
payment at the end of next week. Larkin had to impound
the papers, but my guess is that the executors will be satisfied to have the amount of the check back rather than horse
around with a boat they don't know what to do with."

"My thoughts exactly," Osborne said, and leaned back,
satisfied, his mission accomplished. "Go ahead, Albert. We
haven't got all day."

Carswell, taking no apparent offense at such bluntness,
cleared his throat. "I expect you spent some time with the
Inspector."

"Enough."

"You mentioned Mr. Blake?"

"Certainly."

"And that unpleasantness at the Hall yesterday afternoon? . . . You'll be seeing Mr. Blake later? What I mean is,
I'd like to be sure he intends to go ahead with the purchase.
The way seems clear enough now with no other purchaser
in the picture—"

"I'll make sure, Albert."

Carswell nodded dreamily and the strong Scotch, added
to his pre-luncheon drink, seemed to revive his enthusiasm.

"I worked so long on this that, frankly, I had almost given
up hope of ever bringing it off. The development on Bequia
helped, of course. I can remember when there was nothing
on it but a couple of large coconut plantations; Bastique
was even more remote. The *Antilles* going aground and the
resulting pictures and publicity helped, naturally."

He finished his drink, his thoughts still distant like his
gaze. "The same is true of Young's Island. Nothing there

but some iguanas until those people from England decided to make a swank vacation spot out of it with cottages and pool—"

He stopped and brought his eyes and thoughts into focus when Osborne growled at him again.

"You're still babbling, Albert. Say what you came to say and let's let the man alone."

"Yes, of course." The weak smile was apologetic. "What I hoped you might do for me, Alan, is put in a word with Blake and his company. I had no idea until yesterday of the extent of the development planned. I believe I may have mentioned that I would like to be the local representative. True, I will receive a handsome commission from the Athertons now, but think what it would mean if I could also share in selling the residential lots from time to time as the development progresses."

He leaned forward to put his empty glass on the table and stood up. "Thank you for the drink, Alan. I hope you won't think my request an imposition. Any little word in my behalf will be most appreciated."

Maxwell took a small breath and stood up. How, he asked himself, could you suspect a nice little guy like Carswell of murder? That thought remained with him until after they had gone, until he remembered the things Louise had done to him, and no doubt to others. With her, the rules of normal behavior would not necessarily apply . . .

When Alan Maxwell had beached the dinghy and put the oars back under the veranda he entered the Aquatic Club, the sack with the brandy in one hand. There were a half-dozen visitors on the veranda, tourists by the look of them, having planter's punches, but he went down the length of the dance floor with but one thought in mind.

Two white-shirted boys were talking quietly behind the square bar, and in the hall another was wielding the broom. He wondered if it was the same boy he had noticed when he had first gone aboard the *Annabel* in response to Oscar Jones' frantic appeal. The bar boys could tell him nothing; the sweeper was somewhat more helpful, though not in the beginning when Maxwell asked if he had seen anyone board the *Annabel* at any time during the late morning.

"No, sir," the boy said, leaning on the broom.

"Did you look out there from time to time while you were sweeping?"

The boy refused to meet his eye and Maxwell understood this too. For he had to accept the fact that it was known—the arrival of the police in force was enough to start the questions—that there had been a murder, with a body taken from the ketch. And murder, other than the occasional cutting done in the fields or after an overdose of cheap local rum by a jealous husband or boyfriend, was something so unusual as to fill any native islander with awe and perhaps a private, vicarious fear.

The body had come from the ketch. That ketch belonged to Alan Maxwell. Ergo, maybe the white owner had killed the woman.

"Well," he said, keeping his impatience in check, "did you?"

"Maybe sometimes."

"Did you see anyone in a small boat—you know, like my dinghy?"

"Saw one fisherman."

"Did you see which way he came from?"

The boy shook his head, eyes still averted. "No. Just looked up once and he there."

"Black man or white?"

"Couldn't rightly say, sir. Had a big hat"—he took both hands to fashion an imaginary circle round his head—"like that."

"How was he dressed?"

"Just brown pants and old shirt."

"How close did he get to the *Annabel*?"

The boy thought it over and pointed from his feet to the veranda, a distance of perhaps sixty feet.

"Maybe here to there."

"You didn't see him come?"

"No, sir." This emphatically.

"See him leave?"

"Just look up one time and he gone."

Maxwell nodded and turned away, masking his disappointment and wondering if he had expected too much. For it was, he knew, a perfect way to get aboard the ketch without attracting attention: A fisherman's outfit with a big hat. A short approach from up or down the coast in a skiff easy to come by. Get the ketch between the skiff and the club, make sure the Young's Island launch was not about, and slip aboard. To enter the cabin, doctor the brandy, and be back fishing could be managed in less than two minutes.

"Well, the hell with it," he said aloud and asked for the telephone directory. He looked up the number of Dr. Boy Singh, and when the secretary answered he identified himself and asked if he could speak to the doctor. "Tell him it's urgent, please," he added. "I'll only keep him a minute."

After a brief delay the doctor came on and said in his soft courteous way, "Yes, Mr. Maxwell."

"I have to see you this afternoon, Doctor. Can you work me into your schedule?"

"My nurse said it was urgent. Is there something wrong?"

"Not physically, Doctor. It has to do with my wife and I need your help. Five or ten minutes should be enough."

"This is not a police matter?"

"Not yet. For now it is a routine office call and should be treated as such. Classify it as an emergency. Just see me."

"One moment."

He could hear Singh say something, apparently to the nurse. There was a ten-second pause before he said:

"Very well, Mr. Maxwell. Would four o'clock suit you?"

"Four o'clock would be fine."

13

ALAN MAXWELL WAS JUST crossing the small lobby of the Casurina Inn when the sudden shrilling of the telephone stopped him. He turned, waiting, wondering if someone would answer. When no one appeared after the third ring, he went behind the counter and picked up the phone.

For the past half hour he had been sitting on a bar stool at the club, oblivious of his surroundings and the activity on the veranda. There were no facilities for meals here, but one of the bar boys managed to produce a ham sandwich and he ate automatically, washing it down with a bottle of beer and brooding. Such a mood had little focus and his thoughts centered mostly on how he would approach Dr. Singh and what he would say.

Now the voice that came to him was an instant tonic to the continuing feeling of dismay and uncertainty that had troubled him from the moment Oscar Jones had so abruptly wakened him.

"Alan? . . . Oh, good," Valerie Atherton said. "I tried earlier. I wasn't sure I should, but I've been worried sick. Are you all right?"

"I haven't been arrested yet, if that's what you mean," Maxwell said, warmed with her concern.

"And you actually found your wife's body in your cabin?"

"Oscar did. He came running and got me out of bed."

"Oh, how awful for you. I'm so sorry. Why would anyone do such a thing?"

"If you mean, kill her, I can think of reasons."

"I know, Alan. I meant—"

"I know what you meant and I don't have the answer. I don't think Inspector Larkin does either."

"Was it bad? Did you have a hard time with him?"

He chuckled again at her phrasing. "In the States, we say 'Did he give you a hard time?' . . . No, not really. Very polite, as a matter of fact. Probably a damn sight easier on me—I'll say that for the British-trained police officer—than some tough homicide man back home."

"But he can't think you did it."

"He can't ignore the possibility either. I had all the classic requisites for a prime suspect: motive—a double one—opportunity, inclination, the works."

This time there was a brief silence, and he could imagine her pretty frown and the concerned green eyes as she considered his statement. Then her rebuttal came, curt and convincing.

"That's nonsense and you know it."

"I'm afraid it isn't, Val," he said, and then, to change the subject: "How did you know about her? From Michael?"

"No. I was in bed when he left. He didn't say anything to Mother either. We had no idea anything was wrong until a Captain Andrews drove up in a police car."

"What did he want?"

"Just a statement about our little party at the inn and who was there, and when did we leave, and when was the last time we'd seen your wife, things like that."

"I was with Larkin when Michael came in," Maxwell said. "He admitted they'd had a quarrel and she walked out on him. That's all he'd say . . . How did he seem when he came back to the Hall?"

"Distant, subdued, a stiff-upper-lip attitude. He wouldn't talk about it. Just changed his clothes, called for his horse. He's been in the field ever since."

Her voice seemed to run down as she finished, and he said, "Well, look, Val. When can I see you?"

"Whenever you like."

His first thought, that they have dinner at some out-of-the-way place, he discarded. For somewhere in the back of his brain an idea was taking root. If it flourished sufficiently he could see how he might be busy at dinnertime or a bit later.

"Could we meet somewhere for drinks?"

"I think I'd like that. The atmosphere around here is getting on my nerves. Where and when?"

"How about the Pelican?" he said, and it was not just an idle thought. He had a little business there later; it was also the temporary residence of Leon Carr. "It isn't very fancy, but we can sit on the porch and talk and not run into anyone we know."

"When?"

"Five-thirty? Shall I pick you up?"

"No. The drive will do me good. See you then."

Alan Maxwell was on time when he parked the Consul in the quiet street where Dr. Singh had his home and office. He had changed his clothes once more after talking to Valerie, and he carried the paper bag with its bottle as he went up the steps to the door marked OFFICE.

He was pleased to see the waiting room was empty at this hour. The young, dusky-skinned receptionist recognized him and snapped on the little intercom to announce him.

When she told him he could go right in, he opened the door behind her desk. There were two rooms beyond, both rather small. The first was a sort of consulting room, the second a surgery or examination room. Dr. Singh, behind the desk, rose and nodded, neat, trim, and efficient-looking, the white coat spotless.

Maxwell said, "Good evening," which was the proper expression in spite of the hour, since custom with the local people seemed never to acknowledge a more precise "Good afternoon." He put his bottle bag on the desk and took the chair Singh indicated.

"Did the autopsy tell you anything special?"

"Nothing. I have recovered the bullet and turned it over to the authorities. She was shot fairly close up, from not more than a foot if I'm right about the powder pattern."

He leaned forward, soft eyes curious as Maxwell removed the bottle, and then questioning as he glanced up and Maxwell spoke.

"How are you on toxicology, Doctor?"

"I'm not qualified, if that is what you mean."

"But you had some in medical school."

"In an elementary sort of way."

"I'd like you to take a crack at analyzing this brandy."

"Why?" Singh asked, his manner at once skeptical.

"I think it's poisoned."

The announcement brought the black brows up while things happened behind the dark eyes; but except for the noticeable pause there was little change of expression.

"Why should you think that?"

Maxwell told his story then, his tone flat but intent as he spoke of the overflowing highball and the odd little sip that may have saved his life. By the time he had finished, Singh had uncapped the bottle and was smelling it. Now he stood up, selected a small beaker, and poured out a half-inch of the liquid. Holding it in both hands like a brandy snifter, he took a tentative whiff and then another. He dipped a fingertip, tested, nodded.

"If there *is* poison, we can eliminate one."

"Cyanide? Prussic acid?"

Singh re-capped the bottle and rinsed the beaker. When he turned he wore an odd smile.

"I see you read detective stories too." He sat down, the liquid eyes narrowed in thought, his lips moving absently before he spoke. "I believe I could run tests on the common poisons—arsenic, strychnine, nicotine—"

He reached behind him to remove a fat, impressive-looking volume from a bookshelf.

"This is a universally accepted book on legal medicine written by the Chief Medical Examiner of New York City, the former chief, and a third man holding the same position in the State of New Jersey. There is some information here that would be helpful, a poison section, you might say, with formulas and diagrams for the analysis of the more common ones . . . But why, Mr. Maxwell, if you suspect poisoning, do you not inform Inspector Larkin?"

"Because I'd have to get into something I'd just as soon skip until I know where I stand. I have nothing to support my story. He could think—and I'm not sure I'd blame him— that I set this up myself, a trick to take the heat off me and make him concentrate on someone else . . . Do you see what I mean?"

"I think so."

"I'm asking your help because *I* know damn well some-one—someone who knew my taste for this brandy—doctored that bottle. I'm here as a private patient who needs medical assistance. I'll pay for this visit just as I would for any office call. I expect to be charged for whatever time you spend on the analysis. All I demand is the customary privilege that goes with any doctor-patient relationship."

When Maxwell talked like that you believed him and his obvious sincerity apparently had the same effect on Singh. He allowed himself a small smile.

"You are very convincing, Mr. Maxwell, and I appreciate your position. I will try to help. But as I said, if what we have here is not one of the more common poisons, a sample will have to be sent to Port of Spain or Barbados, where they have facilities and a more qualified man."

"Fair enough." Maxwell breathed an audible sigh of relief as he came to his feet. "And as soon as you can, please, Doctor. I'd even be willing to pay for overtime," he added, his grin crooked. "If you can find out what the poison is, maybe then I can go to Larkin."

He got as far as the door before he thought of something else, and he turned, the grin still there.

"Oh, yes. Perhaps you'd better keep that bottle locked up until you've finished with it in case you have a maid around with a taste for rum."

Singh said he intended to, and Maxwell thanked him again as he left the room.

The Villa Inn was quiet and dozing in the late afternoon sun when Maxwell walked in and went to the bar. A quick glance at the pool end told him there were a couple and a foursome doing some drinking at two tables. He did not order a drink but asked about the Blake party.

"On the beach, I think, Mr. Maxwell," Francis said.

He could see as he started down the winding path that the barman was right. There were eight or ten guests on the cove's tiny beach. A small, thatch-roofed hut with four stools for the convenience of sunbathers served as a bar, but the Blake foursome was closer to the water, the two girls and Tony Russo getting the last of the sun and Sam Blake, hairy-chested and clad in checkered trunks, nursing a drink under an umbrella.

Blake saw him coming. "Hi, Alan," he said, waving his glass, "grab a chair."

Maxwell took the canvas chair between Blake and Russo and gave the two bikini-clad girls a long, appreciative glance. Both were belly down, the straps of their bras unfastened. He could see the soft rounded profile of one breast on the redhead. Both raised slightly to see who the visitor was, and this arching move enhanced the view.

They said hello and the bustier one, the redhead—was this Agnes or Elsie?—put her chin on her folded arms and watched him, the brown eyes slyly curious, as though appraising his modest good looks and net worth. The blonde brushed the straight hair—and from this angle he could see that deep in the part it was darker—out of her eyes, and he decided that her prettiness had a more practiced, artful look than that of her companion. Russo, examining his empty glass, yelled for the waiter.

"We figured they had you in the pokey," he said, his tone sardonic and the dark flat eyes inscrutable as always.

"We wondered when you'd be around," Blake said. "What are you drinking?"

"Nothing, thanks," Maxwell said, lighting a cigarette. "I couldn't make it before. Were the police here?"

"An Inspector Larkin."

"He was cute too," said the redhead, and Maxwell remembered this was Agnes. "A nifty uniform and a swagger stick—isn't that what you call them, Tony?"

Russo touched his mustache absently but made no reply, and Blake said, "You must have had quite a day. You found her body in the cabin, hunh? But she wasn't killed there? Do the cops know where yet?"

"In her bungalow. Last night, sometime between nine and eleven, according to the medical examiner. They found two shells on the floor. A .25 automatic, they think."

"A dame's gun," Russo said.

"Did she have one?" Blake asked.

"She did at one time."

"How come they let you out, Maxwell?" Russo accepted his fresh drink, another rum punch by the looks of it, and took an appreciative swallow. "You had the motive. She hated your guts. You could have sneaked out after she left the Atherton guy—"

"So could you," Maxwell said, beginning to burn at the other's needling and insolent attitude. "You just said you saw her leave." He turned to Blake to cool off. "What did they want from you?"

"Who we saw, where we went, and when." Blake's eyes narrowed slightly and his chin tipped about an inch. "I guess you told the cops about our deal and how your wife tried to louse us up."

"I had to, didn't I? It seemed like a good idea to point out I wasn't the only one with a motive."

"You figure a motive for us?" Russo said nastily. "How?"

"She outbid you on Bastique."

"We could have matched it Monday."

"She could have upped the offer again. She could afford it."

"The Athertons could be made to accept our offer. We could sue the—"

"Sure. And maybe two years later you'd get a favorable court ruling."

"Balls!"

"I'm not going to be a hypocrite," Blake said, ignoring the argument, "and say I'm sorry. About your wife, I mean. I doubt if you are either, if you're honest with yourself. She was out to get you—boat, architect's job for us, the works. She didn't want Bastique; she just wanted to screw you."

Maxwell knew there was a lot of truth in this. He accepted Blake's summing-up, but he was still thinking about Russo.

"Where were you when my wife was killed, anyway?"

"How do I know when she was killed?" Russo said. "That steel band was driving us out of our skulls with all that pounding, so we cut out."

"Went to bed, huh?"

"Doesn't everybody?"

"With a perfect alibi beside you."

Russo's mustached lip twisted, and his dark eyes were bright and mean. He put down his glass and leaned forward in his chair.

"Listen, you—"

"You listen!" Maxwell said, his gaze steady, and half-hoping the other would start something. He had started to rise when Blake stopped him.

"Knock it off! Both of you."

"Sure," Maxwell said and felt the tension go out of him. "Just tell me this, was this character born nasty or has he been working on it for some time?"

Blake chuckled softly, unperturbed. An unexpected glint of approval showed in the hooded eyes, and Maxwell knew then that while Russo might talk tough and possibly supply the muscle, it was Blake who called the shots and made them stick. He also was ready to admit that if Blake felt certain measures were necessary, his orders would probably be carried out.

"Tony was born mean," he said, still amused. "He's okay when he watches his mouth; he has his uses."

"He's not always mean," a small voice said, and Maxwell saw the blond Elsie smirking at him.

Russo glared and said, "Shut up!" and the girl made a face behind his back.

"The fact is," Blake said, his tone again businesslike, "we've got our deal. Too bad about your wife—I guess—but we're the only bidders now and our option stands. We wrap it up Monday. I've already been on the phone to old lady Atherton. The *Annabel* ready to go?"

"She'll be ready. Whether I go with her is something else."

Blake knew what he meant. "You figure the head man down at CID is going to say no? You didn't kill her, did you? Unless he can nail you, why should he stop you from sailing to Bastique? There's no place to go from there. He could have you picked up any time."

Maxwell said he hoped it worked out that way, and Blake asked about provisions and liquor.

"I'll be all set by Monday noon," Maxwell said. "I'll have the cook at the Pelican bake a ham and roast a piece of beef for me. Maybe roast a couple of chickens and take a couple frozen along for Oscar to fricassee."

"Sure," Blake said with some enthusiasm. "I remember he makes good biscuits. I'd like some fish too the way he fixes them. We should be able to snag some, shouldn't we? The girls have nothing to do. While you and Tony and me are tramping around and checking out the big house, your mate can take the girls fishing."

"Could we?" Elsie said with a little squeal, coming up on her elbows and arching her back, and either forgetting that her young breasts were almost completely exposed or not caring.

Apparently Russo did. "Cover up!" he snarled. "Before it all falls out."

"I'd like to," Agnes said dreamily, tugging absently at her well-filled bandeau. "I've never been fishing."

Maxwell smiled at her and gave her a slow wink, aware that he was beginning to like both girls, and their obvious innocence in certain areas. The gesture brought a friendly grin, and very deliberately then she winked back, the mascaraed lashes fanning out across the pink cheek . . . Sensing that Blake had said something about liquor, he said:

"What did you have in mind?"

"Scotch for me. With vodka, if they have it here, or gin, for bloody marys. Rum for Tony. The girls will drink anything and—"

"I like gin-and-tonic," Agnes said, still smiling at Maxwell.

"All right. Couple cases of tonic, two or three cases of

Heineken, okay? . . . I've been thinking," Blake added, warming to his subject, "how about canceling further charters if you can? When we start moving men and things we can use the ketch full-time. We'll work something out, hunh?"

"You'll need a native schooner for your small dozers and shovels—"

"Sure, sure. And check out this cement-block guy. He'll have to expand, and we can help with capital for a piece of the operation."

He went on with other items, but Maxwell was no longer listening. When he glanced at his watch he saw it was time to move on and stood up. He said he had to run and if Blake wanted him for anything to leave word at the Casurina Inn.

14

ALAN MAXWELL WAS EARLY for his date with Valerie Atherton at the Pelican Hotel because he had some things to do. He went first to the second-floor lobby, a light and airy room with two exposures and odd tables and wicker chairs. There was no reception desk as such, but a small bar which did double duty. The register was somewhere underneath and the key and message rack was tacked to the wall nearby so the guests could use the appropriate boxes on a self-service basis.

The bar was strictly for service, with no stools provided. You sat where you liked and gave your order to a waiter, and eventually—sometimes you had to run downstairs for Marvin, the clerk-barman—you would be served. Now, at a few minutes after five, Maxwell was glad to see that Marvin was in attendance. He had an elbow on the bartop, his palm supporting his chin, and he seemed half-asleep until Maxwell stopped in front of him.

He was a small, slow-moving Negro of indeterminate age with a large mouth that showed nearly all his teeth when he smiled. Away from the hotel, he liked to fish, and twice in the past when the *Annabel* had been tied up at one of the town piers, Maxwell had got out the five-horsepower outboard and let Marvin take the dinghy for harbor fishing. He was about to use these past favors as leverage now if he had to.

"What do you say, Marvin?"

Marvin grinned and straightened up. "Can't say, sir."

"Police been here today?"

"That's right," Marvin said, some new interest showing. "But they don't bother me none."

"They wanted to see Mr. Carr, right?"

"Right."

"Did they talk to him out here?"

"In his room." Marvin waved to the long hall on his right.

"Do you make him plenty of drinks?"

"Only some. Mostly he drink in the downstairs bar."

"Does he eat dinner here often?"

"Not often. Mostly he go out. Must come back late 'cause I don't see him much, nights."

"Is he there now? . . . Okay," he said when Marvin nodded. "I want to look over his room when he leaves this evening. I'll be outside. When I'm sure he's gone I'll come up and you'll unlock the door for me."

Marvin's eyes bulged, and he recoiled visibly from the thought. "Couldn't do that, Mister Max, sir."

"Why not?"

"Get fired."

"Not if nobody knows but me. I'll give you two choices: I come in and give you the word, you go down, unlock the door, come back. Or you pretend you don't see me take Carr's key and I'll do the unlocking. Who's to know?"

Marvin remained unconvinced, the worry still showing. To give him a nudge, Maxwell said:

"You like to use my dinghy and outboard, don't you?"

"I really do," Marvin said honestly, beginning to weaken.

"Did you ever do anything for me about those other times, like give me a free drink or something?"

Marvin shrugged and showed his white teeth again. He

glanced about the empty room to make sure there were no eavesdroppers.

"We work it out."

"That's better, Marvin. Much better. You know Miss Atherton, don't you?"

"Oh, yes, sir."

"Well, if she comes in before I get back, ask her to wait for me on the porch, okay?"

The street-level bar of the Pelican was the one that did the business—a dim, uninviting room that smelled of rum and beer and stale smoke. Not a place to take your best girl, it was respectable enough, and very handy for seamen off the cargo ships that tied up from time to time.

At the moment there were perhaps a dozen customers, most of them lined up at a long bar presided over by a husky six-footer with a noticeable scar along the hinge of one jaw. He recognized Maxwell and nodded as he went past on his way to the kitchen. He had tried several hotel cooks in town to prepare meats for charters, and had found Alexander—no last name that he knew of—not only the best but one who could be trusted to do the shopping. He knew meat better than Maxwell, and whatever rakeoff he got was reasonable.

He told the cook what he had in mind and watched him make notes on a paper bag. He handed over some money and asked if it was enough.

Alexander nodded and slipped the bills under his apron. "Too late to buy today. Best I cook Monday morning."

Maxwell agreed. "I wouldn't be picking it up before Monday noon anyway."

Maxwell was on the veranda when he saw Valerie park her car. The Pelican was on a corner, giving a partial view of two streets, a section of the harbor, and, in the distance, the rugged silhouette of Bequia. Now he leaned over the railing as she approached. She looked up when he called, and gave him her nice smile and a comradely wave.

He was waiting for her at the top of the stairs. Two couples in tourist garb, complete with cameras and light-meters, were having drinks at a lobby table and Maxwell guided the girl past them to the veranda. When Marvin appeared, she said she'd have a gin-and-tonic and Maxwell said to make it two.

She put her straw bag, the sort that seemed indigenous to most of the islands, on the table, and placed her dark glasses beside it.

"Well," she said, the green eyes bright with undisguised curiosity, "what can you tell me?"

"Not much."

"Who have you seen since we talked?"

"I stopped to see Sam Blake and friends." He grinned. "You remember seeing the two little dolls last night, don't you?"

She made a face and said, "I do indeed, and that awful man Russo. Ugh." She looked at him with one eye and then with both. "Those dolls, as you call them, aren't wives?"

"I doubt it."

"Why?"

"Too young, at least for Blake."

"They brought them all the way from Boston and they're sharing bungalows. My goodness," she said, not at all shocked and unable to stifle her interest. "What are they like?"

"Not bad. A blonde and a redhead. Not more than twenty or twenty-one. Gorgeous figures and pretty faces in a bland, artificial sort of way, probably with empty heads."

"Not hard?"

"Not the way you mean. At least, it doesn't show."

"What do you think they do? I mean when they're home?"

"Probably models, aspiring actresses or entertainers, with some occasional call girl business on the side."

"You mean they were paid to come?"

Maxwell laughed. "Of course. Frankly, I think they're having a ball. They're getting a free ten-day vacation in the sun for being nice and agreeable, and Blake will probably slip them five hundred or a thousand bucks—whatever they agreed on in the beginning."

They waited while Marvin served the drinks and slipped away. She said: "Cheers," and hiked her chair a little closer, still full of talk, as though compelled by some vicarious excitement that had to be satisfied.

"You don't know anything more, Alan? Inspector Larkin hasn't been around again? Have you any idea what the police think?" She watched him shake his head. "I've never known anyone who was murdered, or even someone who knew someone who was. When I heard what happened this morning it was as if I'd read some account in a newspaper. I'm sorry for her, naturally, but only as I would be for anyone I didn't really know.

"She was a complete stranger to me," she went on, "and I couldn't possibly like her from what you told me and the exhibition she put on yesterday afternoon . . . Poor Michael," she said, her mental gears shifting without warning. "Actually it's all for the good, don't you think? When he gets his senses back and has a chance to think he'll know it's really Wanda he loves, just as she loves him.

"The trouble with him," she added with some irritation, "is that he needs a built-in self-starter. He's so nice and decent, and so damn slow to get going. And Wanda's not aggressive enough. She should have got him into bed. She should know enough to manage that; any woman should, don't you think?"

She was so serious in her dissertation that Maxwell had to laugh. "Talk about your predatory females."

"Of course, I was frightfully upset about you," she continued, as though she hadn't heard. "I still am—"

"Are you sure you didn't think I'd finally blown my top?"

"Don't be silly," she said in sharp reproval. "You couldn't kill anyone."

"Certainly I could, so could anyone given proper provocation. There were times when we were married that I wondered why I didn't. Premeditated murder?" he said, half to himself. "No. I don't think I could do that, ever. But the way it looks to me—and the police too, I think—there was no premeditation last night in that bungalow."

"Oh—they know for sure that's where it happened?"

He told her about the two empty shells the police had found there and the possibility that the automatic used might have been his wife's.

"But the police didn't find it?"

"Not while I was there."

"Then whoever killed her must still have it."

"If he didn't throw it into the sea."

"So now what happens?" she said, a slight frown beginning to crease the smooth brows. "Do you have to sit and wait until the police decide to question you again?"

"I have one small and probably useless thought," he said and told her about his idea of searching Leon Carr's room.

"Oh, my goodness!" she said with quick concern. "Why would you want to do that?"

"Well, for one thing, someone ran off with two very valuable pieces of jewelry. They were gone when the police searched the bungalow."

The frown deepened as she remained unconvinced.

"But won't the police already have searched the room, I mean Carr's? And what if you're caught?"

"Sure they've searched it. Carr knows that. He could think they won't try again . . . If I'm stupid enough to get caught," he added, considering the possibility before he smiled and reassured her, "I suppose I might get pinched. But at least it's a bailable offense."

She did not share in his easy dismissal of the subject, and

gradually he found her doubts infectious. He tried to force himself to be honest, to ask why the idea of such a search seemed so important.

Just what the hell am I looking for? he thought.

Not the jewelry or traveler's checks, not really. Then what? He came up with the best answer he could think of.

"I guess I just want to know more about the guy. I never thought too much about him before. Maybe there's something in his room or bags that will give me a clue. Sure, I'm grabbing at straws, but if he got in a jam with Louise or gave her a hard time or—Oh, I don't know," he said unable to be more specific. "It's just that at times she could make any man turn to murder."

He realized she was no longer looking at him, her gaze remote now and oddly troubled.

"Even Michael?"

That one stopped him. He had not expected it, but he could understand what prompted it. That possibility, remote as it must have seemed to her, had to be considered, and she wanted assurance. He was further surprised when she read his thoughts and said:

"Don't tell me you haven't thought about it."

"All right," he said, gambling that he could be honest and get away with it. "Because I knew Louise so well, I'd say he could have, but—"

"Do you think he did?"

"You didn't let me finish. I said *could* because I still think the murder was a spur-of-the moment action. They'd quarreled and she walked out on him in a huff—and anytime Louise was in a huff, it was some production—but he maintains that he did not follow her to her bungalow."

"Go on," she said, her tone suggesting he tread lightly.

He shrugged and made an unsuccessful attempt to take her hand. "Maybe that's the truth and maybe it isn't. What I'll never believe is that he would even think of coming back later and taking the body to the ketch in some mistaken attempt to involve me. From what I know of your brother, he wouldn't run or hide if he killed someone, or try to put the blame on an innocent person; he'd stand and take his lumps like a man."

He could see the subtle change in her eyes as he finished, the slight fall of her breasts as she let her breath out slowly.

"Yes," she said softly. "I think he probably would." Then, as though reassured by his reply and weary of the subject, she digressed without warning. "I guess the Bastique development will go right ahead now, won't it?"

"From what Blake said this afternoon, yes."

"Then you'll be down here more or less permanently?"

"Not the way I see it."

"Oh?"

"I never expected to be here permanently, not from the first. I ran away from something, but I knew I'd have to go back some day."

"But if you're to be the architect—"

"I'm going to do the inn and cottages"—this time she let him capture her hand—"and stick around until they're finished. Say a year or a little longer. Eventually they'll need plans for private residences when they start selling lots. They'll have to set certain standards so people can't put up any old kind of house.

"What I hope to do is make a deal with Blake and his company to design and furnish working drawings of maybe three basic layouts," he said. "Basic but flexible, so each design can be modified with simple and easy to make alterations, so that no two houses will look exactly alike. I'd be willing to do these on speculation if the company would give me a flat fee each time one was used. That way it would be a lot cheaper for the buyer than if he had to furnish his own plans, and at the same time it would be something that the developers could approve."

He stopped then, aware somehow that there had been a subtle change in the girl. Her hand remained passive under his own, but the green eyes held a certain misty glow he had never seen before. She seemed somehow not to be aware of this look and made no attempt to avoid his own steady scrutiny.

For perhaps another five seconds they seemed unconsciously transfixed by the spell as some new excitement grew in Maxwell's brain and he knew something wonderful was happening.

With it came a pleasant inner stirring, a surge of emotion that was new and startling and wholly unexpected. Swiftly then the conviction grew and he finally understood what it was. Ten minutes earlier the thought may have been there but so dormant that he would not have recognized it. Now he knew what had happened with a certainty and conviction that could no longer be denied.

He was in love with Valerie. Totally and completely.

She was the one who broke the spell; he saw it happen, could almost see her think as she realized what she had been doing. Her quick smile brought back the friendly brightness of her eyes and her mood was gone. She removed her hand and glanced at her wristwatch and he spoke quickly.

"Now you tell *me* something. Had you planned to spend the rest of your life here? I don't mean St. Vincent necessarily, but Barbados, or anywhere in the area?"

She tipped her chin slightly and shook her head. "I don't think so. I hadn't really thought too much about it."

"Then you wouldn't *have* to stay around? I mean, because of your mother or brother or the estate?"

"Of course not. Mother wouldn't expect me to, so long as she had Michael."

"You know Boston. Could you see yourself living there? Like having a home?"

She was smiling now. She knew what he meant and she was not about to slip back into her previous mood or be pinned down. She felt her still-windblown coppery hair and looked him right in the eye, her expression secretly amused and somewhat challenging.

"Why not? Boston, New York, Canada. Just so long as I could come back here for a week or two once a year—perhaps twice, if it could be managed."

Maxwell found he could match her smile.

"Just do me one favor."

"If I can."

"Don't go falling in love with that hotel guy in Barbados. I mean, not for a while. Okay?"

She did not answer and he had expected none. The smile was still there as she glanced at her watch and said she had to run.

"Where?" he asked, masking his disappointment.

"I'm picking up Wanda. She's coming for dinner, believe it or not. Mother—she just won't give up with her matchmaking—talked her into it. She said Wanda owed it to her and Michael to help him get through the next couple of days."

She chuckled and said, "You should have heard her try to convince Wanda—and I guess she did—that Michael's brief affair was nothing but a thoughtless fling, a silly infatuation that all men had to go through. Anyway, she's coming. Just the four of us. Maybe it will be good for Michael. And I'll be there to keep Wanda trying."

"Have you talked to him yet?"

She shook her head again. "He was still out in the fields when I left. If he's not back soon, Mother'll get her horse and go get him."

She picked up her straw bag and slipped on the sunglasses. As he rose with her she kissed him on the cheek, and then caught her breath as some new thought came to her.

"I almost forgot. You're expected tomorrow afternoon as usual. Mother wouldn't think of letting a minor matter like murder interfere with her schedule. Custom must be observed at all costs."

Maxwell knew what she meant. Sunday afternoon tea at the Hall was a must and apparently had been for twenty years. More recently, cocktails had become available and two dressing rooms had been added near the pool for those who liked a dip first. The number of guests varied from eight or ten to twenty or more, depending on Dorothy Atherton's whim. He knew, however, that he would never have been invited to the command performance if he hadn't met Valerie; in fact, he was only permitted to attend on the weekends she spent at home.

Now, when she had thanked him for the drink he walked to the car with her. The last thing she said to him came as a word of both warning and assurance.

"If you get caught tonight," she said mischievously, "have the Inspector phone me and I'll come down and bail you out."

15

LEON CARR CAME OUT of the downstairs entrance to the Pelican Hotel sometime before eight. Maxwell was not sure just when, because he did not care. It was quite dark and had been for the past fifteen minutes or so, and he had been sitting in the Consul parked diagonally across the paving on the sea side of the street, thinking wryly of the times he had seen a similar scene in television dramas.

He remembered that what he was doing was called a stake-out, and he had often sneered at the miraculous and providential coincidence that enabled the detective, or villain, if that was the case, to find a convenient observation point on a supposedly busy city street—in reality, a set built on the back lot of a movie company—and be ready at all times to take up the chase, unhampered by traffic or obstacles of any kind.

Here it had been easy. There was no traffic to speak of. The country people had done their buying and selling and were long gone, safely in their shacks and cottages, the windows closed against the night air. The downstairs bar was doing a good business, calypso records booming their rhythms from the jukebox. Otherwise the street here under the trees was quiet and deserted, and when he saw Carr

get in his car, make a U-turn, and head up the coast he had
an idea the man would be dining at the Villa Inn for the
Saturday night soiree to do a bit of drinking and perhaps
cut in on some of the local ladies.

Maxwell had eaten well if not fancily at a small table
tucked in the far corner of the Pelican bar, which did not
ordinarily serve food. The atmosphere was typical, with the
ever-present jukebox and a laughing, shouting clientele
nearly one hundred percent black.

He had earned his spot because of the amount of charter-
boat orders he gave the chef; and the food, the same that
went upstairs by dumbwaiter to the regular dining room,
was as good as any on the island. Tonight he'd had soup,
not otherwise named and therefore *du jour*, which contained chunks of what would have been lobster in Boston
but was more like *langouste*; broiled dolphin and French
fries; coconut ice cream, and chocolate cake.

Now, as he crossed the street, he had not the slightest
feeling of doubt or apprehension about what he intended
to do. He mounted the stairs with confidence, to find Marvin in his customary pose: half-leaning on the counter and
half-asleep. He could see then that there were two couples
on the darkened veranda; noise from the dining room told
him others had not finished.

When he woke Marvin up, he said, "You going to unlock
it for me?"

Marvin gave a silent but emphatic shake of his head and
then pointed with his chin at the key rack. "Last room on
the right," he said. "Number fourteen."

The Pelican had only two rooms with private baths and
Carr's was one of these, a corner room with two windows
for slightly better ventilation. There was no one in the hall
when Maxwell fitted the key and unlocked the door. He
slipped it back into his jacket pocket, took a final over-the-
shoulder look, and then opened the door. There would be a
switch for the overhead light just inside, but he did not

want that much illumination flooding the hall as he entered. When he spotted the small lamp on the table desk on his left, he closed the door behind him and felt his way across the darkness until he touched the desk.

His fingers slid up the wooden lamp base and found the pushbutton. He pressed it, and as a soft glow flooded the room, he turned to take a step. Apparently something rather heavy and boxlike had been placed beside one of the table legs, because it caught the tip of his shoe and threw him off balance. He stumbled awkwardly, not going down but lurching sideways, and it was at this instant that he heard the shot.

Instinct and healthy reflexes took over then. There was no time to think but somehow he was full length on the floor and practically flat on his face, wondering if he'd actually heard the *thunk* of the slug as it smacked into the wall, before or after the blast.

Not that it was loud. It had a flat, snapping quality that told him it had come from outside. The following silence was broken by a rapid thudding sound, and he wondered if someone was coming down the hall until he realized it was his heart. The simple knowledge that he was still alive was curiously uplifting, and seconds later his brain was functioning with a cold and calculating precision.

He knew he had not been hit, that the unseen object he had tripped over had probably saved him. He also knew what he had to do.

For the layout of the room and its surroundings was already blueprinted in his mind. There was nothing behind the building, but directly opposite the side window was a similar two-story structure housing a garage on the street floor and some offices above. There was, he knew, a gap of six or eight feet between the two walls, and the gunman must have been waiting on the opposite rooftop for his target to turn on the light. Since the rooftops were about the same height, he was safe so long as he stayed down, and he began to breathe again as a surging anger smoothed the ragged edges of his nerves.

Pivoting crablike on his belly, he kept squirming until he faced the desk. He saw the typewriter case that had saved him and, just beyond it, the wall socket. Three more feet of belly-crawling enabled him to reach the lamp cord. A quick yank and a welcome blackness blanketed the room.

Hunched over now and moving towards the open window, he felt his way past the end of the bed, then slid along the wall to the window frame. He peered cautiously round it, identified the flat line of the other roof, and saw nothing but blue-black sky, patches of clouds that seemed iridescent at the edges, with clear, star-studded openings in between.

It came as no surprise to find the rooftop empty. He looked a long time, eyes straining, but nothing moved. Finally he straightened, took a good deep breath, and found the cord that regulated the cheap Venetian blind. He let it flop to the sill, closed the plastic slats, groped back across the room to the desk. When he realized he would be wasting time looking for the lamp cord and plug, he continued to the door and the wall switch and flicked on the overhead light.

The room, as he had expected, was just another inexpensive hotel room, much like his own, but somewhat larger: a double bed with a mosquito net hanging tentlike for a few feet and then knotted out of the way by the maid. A chest, a dresser with mirror, the table desk, and a straight chair; a wicker chair and one floor lamp.

The closet held no surprises. He saw that his palms were still sweaty, but his nerves were under control and an irresistible stubbornness was building steadily inside him as he searched the pockets of the tropical worsted suit, the checked madras jacket, the three pairs of summer-weight slacks, one plaid and two plain-colored. When he found the two suitcases empty, he continued his examination of the drawers in the chest and dresser. There he found two .35

millimeter cameras, one German and one Japanese, an
equipment case with filters, a light meter, two extra lenses
of different focal lengths, a flash unit.

It was the drawer of the table desk that interested him
most. This, it seemed, was Carr's business drawer, and as he
went over the various items he began to get a picture of
what the investigator had been doing and how he stood.

A checkbook on a Boston bank, assuming the subtraction
was correct, showed a balance of $1387.40. A manila folder
with carbons of reports also held a copy of the memoran-
dum on the original agreement that had been made with
Louise Maxwell. The initial payment or retainer had been
for $1,000, and the terms stated that she was to pay $600
a week for Carr's services plus all reasonable expenses.

A hotel bill from the Barbados Hilton along with certain
itemized expenses showed that Carr had done very well for
himself during his week's stay there, particularly in the
drinks and miscellaneous categories. There were similar
itemized expense statements for the weeks spent here in
Kingstown, but no record of any further payment from
Carr's employer. The weekly reports also gave a rather accurate picture of Maxwell's activities, present and past,
along with the status of his mortgage held by George Osborne.

When he finally shut the drawer and stood up, his sense
of failure and dissatisfaction did nothing to brighten his
mood, and he was now forced to agree with Valerie Atherton's evaluation of the venture. The whole thing was a bust
and, but for a bit of luck, could have been a fatal one. There
were no hidden jewels or traveler's checks; he knew very
little more about Carr than he had already suspected. As he
started to brood about the gunman who had been waiting
on the roof, his common sense finally told him such brooding could just as well be done in his car.

With the light off and a furtive glance into the corridor
to be certain it was empty, he left the room, locking the

door behind him. There was no Marvin dozing behind the desk this time; there was, in fact, no one to be seen as he slipped the key into the proper slot and descended the stairs to the sidewalk.

Once in his car, he did not drive off immediately and before he could start to analyze the situation, he suddenly realized that some new nervousness had begun to work on him in the form of a delayed reaction, and for the first time he really felt scared.

At the time of the shot he had been too busy to be frightened. Surprise, bewilderment, consternation, and the desperate effort to stay alive had kept him too occupied to think then of what might have happened if luck, fate, and his own clumsiness had not all been on his side.

Slowly then his anger and resentment got him past the spasm of fear, and he began to ask himself questions.

How, he thought in sudden fury, could the unknown gunman have known he would be coming to the Pelican in the first place?

He answered that one by admitting that it could have been possible for anyone looking for him, say that afternoon, to have eventually found him at the hotel. His meeting with Valerie could have been observed, and the observer could have known that Maxwell had had his meal there and had then gone back to the car. Eventually he would have seen him enter—

He stopped abruptly, knowing finally that such reasoning was specious. Assuming all these things were possible, there could still have been no way for the gunman to know that he was going to Leon Carr's room.

To get a more acceptable premise, he put himself in the other's place. Such a man would not risk going to the roof until dark, and complete darkness had only just become a fact when Carr had left the hotel . . .

It came to him then, and he wondered how he could have missed the only likely solution. Probably, he thought, because until this moment of revelation he had been concerned only with himself, a state easily conditioned by the previous attempt to poison him.

Sure. It was Carr who was the intended victim.

The gunman had stationed himself in the proper spot a few minutes after Carr had left, prepared to wait until his victim entered his room and turned on the light. That this happened long before he had any reason to expect Carr's return would make no difference to a man bent on murder.

A light had gone on in the proper room. A target had presented itself and in his eagerness to kill he had fired at once.

Satisfied that it could have happened no other way, Maxwell started the car. As he let out the clutch and began to roll, he was aware of one more thought that had seeped into his consciousness to give him trouble.

The killer must now know that he had failed—for a dead man could not switch off a light.

16

Maxwell was sitting in his room clad only in undershorts when the double knock came at the door. A glance at his watch told him it was 11:36, and this reminded him that he had been sitting there brooding for close to two hours.

The episode at the Pelican had taken a lot out of him and as much as he tried, it was impossible to dismiss completely his own narrow escape. He had fixed a bowl of ice downstairs when he came in and brought a small pitcher of water with it—sugarcane brandy and water was a pleasant analgesic—and he did not force things but took it easy and smoked too many cigarettes.

Now, not knowing whom he might find outside in the hall and not particularly caring, he reached for the doorknob.

The sight of the police constable standing so straight and proper aroused only a mild feeling of surprise, his only reaction being some curiosity as to why Inspector Larkin had not bothered him before.

The constable touched the visor of his cap politely. He was in his night uniform, a heavy-looking creation, blue-black with red stripes running down the sides of the long trousers. Such an outfit made little sense to Maxwell and seemed always to be an unnecessary hazard. For such offi-

cers still patroled on foot in certain areas and rode bicycles
in others, so it always startled the hell out of him to come
upon one at the side of the road, because the black face and
dark uniform set against a black night made a car's headlights seem inadequate indeed. Custom, he supposed.

"Yes?"

"Inspector Larkin says you are to come with me, sir."

The sir was very broad indeed, but the words had a precise and properly efficient connotation.

Maxwell took a long-suffering breath and expelled it deliberately. He glanced down at his near-nakedness, finger-
combed his unruly dark hair, considered the two inches of
drink that remained in his glass.

"I don't suppose he told you why?"

"No, sir. The message came by radio only minutes ago
while we are in Calliaqua."

Maxwell nodded and sighed again. "All right, Constable.
Do you want to come in while I put on some clothes or—"

"I will wait outside, sir." He reached forward as he spoke
and politely closed the door.

Maxwell put on what he had taken off two hours earlier,
poured water from the large white pitcher into the matching bowl. He washed his face and combed his hair, checked
the cigarettes in his pocket, and, almost as an afterthought,
swallowed the last of his drink.

He led the way down the dimly lighted stairs and back
across the similarly lighted lobby to the back hall. A police
car with its lights on stood in the parking area. On the left
was a low row of buildings containing the kitchen and servants' quarters. The door was open in one of these and a
maid in a dark robe, ignoring the unhealthy night air, had
ventured out. The driver had walked over and now they
were talking softly, thereby putting the maid in the envi-
able position of being able to pass along to her co-workers
whatever bits of gossip she had picked up.

At a call from Maxwell's escort, the driver came back to the car and got behind the wheel. When Maxwell had been motioned into the rear seat they rolled up the incline to the coast road and turned left.

Maxwell leaned back and lit a cigarette, determined not to speculate as to the reason for the radio demand that he be picked up. On the other hand, the deep-seated and lingering resentment, the residue of his anger at the one who had fired at him in Leon Carr's room, had been stimulated rather than diminished by the two or three—or was it four? —drinks he had been nursing. His ineffectual efforts to do something constructive did nothing to improve his frame of mind, but served only to aggravate his already smouldering thoughts.

Now his gaze followed the headlights as they went up and down and around the narrow crowned road. The night seemed much darker somehow, and he wondered about this until he recalled the slice of new moon which had been up earlier, and realized it had set.

Few lights showed by the roadside and none at all in the poorer homes. Then the town and harbor spread below as they descended, and he could make out the two freighters tied up at the docks and the other one at anchor farther out in the roadstead. The downtown streets seemed empty now as they continued westward, slowing down some as they turned in among the warehouses. Another sharp right took them into the alleyway between two such buildings, and Maxwell sat up when he saw the activity ahead.

He could not identify the parked vehicles at first, because their headlights were shining towards him, and he sat where he was while the two constables stepped down. A few seconds later someone opened a rear door, and he identified the neat, well-dressed figure of Inspector Larkin, in plainclothes now, his dark suit and ebony face nearly merging with the night.

"Thank you for coming, Mr. Maxwell," he said. "There is something I wish to show you."

Maxwell followed somewhat blindly until he had passed the glare of the headlights and then he could make out a familiar sedan with both doors open on one side, a small van-type ambulance; two other dark sedans like the one he had just left had pulled some distance ahead.

There was a blanket-covered stretcher on wheels near the open rear doors of the ambulance, the outline of the still form beneath it unmistakable. Only then could Maxwell understand that someone else must have been killed that evening and his first reaction was one of wonderment rather than surprise.

He could see Dr. Singh close his black bag and say something to the ambulance attendants. He would have liked to speak to the doctor, if only briefly, to ask if he had made any progress in isolating the poison but he knew this was not the time. Instead, he simply stood there, conscious of other details now, forcing himself to accept the fact that this was not a bad dream or something born of fantasy. Gray walls with high sliding doors stretched far ahead, and he realized he did not know quite where he was. The overhead sky was black and cloudless now, and it was strangely quiet until the doctor entered his car and slammed the door.

By then he could see two other men, apparently plainclothesmen, working half inside the sedan nearest the right wall, and a uniformed constable standing guard at the far end. Once again Maxwell tried not to speculate. He made a conscious effort to keep his mind blank until he felt Larkin's hand on his arm. They moved slowly, automatically, toward the ambulance and stopped short of the stretcher.

"A bit of luck that we discovered this before morning," Larkin said by way of explanation. "A patrol car turned down here about a half hour ago. Probably trying to sneak a smoke," he added dryly, "but no matter. That sedan you see had no business here, so they stopped and turned a

torch on it. According to Dr. Singh, death probably occurred sometime after ten."

"And I suppose," Maxwell said flatly, "you want to know
what I've been doing all evening."

"Among other things, yes. However, there is something
else I thought you ought to see before the body was removed; that's why I wanted you here as soon as possible.
First, let me ask you something. Who do you think is beneath that blanket?"

Because the question was unexpected, it brought a sudden onrush of irritation that he could not entirely control.

"This is a guessing game now? How many chances do I
get?"

Larkin ignored the sarcasm. "If my methods seem unorthodox, I have my reasons. As I believe I mentioned this
morning, you are our principal suspect, and it is my duty to
question you as such. But you suggested that there were
others who knew your wife who may have had equally
valid motives."

Maxwell thought it over, but not for long, aware now that
the self-imposed blocking of his mind on the ride to town
had been no more than a feeble attempt to avoid a mental
commitment. He had tried to lull himself into an attitude of
indifference—he wondered if the drinks were responsible—
and now he had to face again the cold hard fact of murder.

For he *knew* who was under that blanket. The episode at
the Pelican and his certainty that Leon Carr was the intended victim seemed to leave no alternative, but for some
reason he was reluctant to come right out and say so without quibbling.

"If you want a hunch," he said with ill-concealed reluctance, "I'll give you a name."

"Very well."

"Leon Carr."

"Why?"

"I told you. A hunch."

Larkin wouldn't let go. "Based on what?"

"On the fact that I know there were times last night at the Villa Inn when Carr wasn't in the main room. I missed him at least once that I remember because I saw him come back to the bar. He was definitely absent for a while. He could've easily gone to the bungalow. If he worked for my wife there was always a possibility that he might get in trouble with her, and I know how she could react and how violent she could get when something displeased her. If she got the idea Carr was cheating her or holding out and if—"

He stopped abruptly, his annoyance mushrooming and his temper on the ragged edge.

"What the hell!" he said harshly. "Why should *I* bother to figure it? You're the policeman."

"So I am," Larkin said with his customary poise. "And you made a point with which I can agree."

"What point?"

"Mr. Carr twice left the Villa Inn last night. The second time for several minutes."

"You've been questioning the help?"

"Everyone who could possibly know something including the drivers out in the parking lot. We have not been able to locate quite all of them who might have been there . . ."

Maxwell didn't hear the rest of it, because in that same moment he became aware of his own vulnerable position. *Oh, brother!* he thought. *Those damn drivers! What if one of them saw me?*

Larkin's voice brought him back: "Your guess was a good one, Mr. Maxwell. Mr. Carr *was* in that sedan—his own, the one he was renting—with two bullets in the side of his chest.

"It would seem," he added thoughtfully, "that he had agreed to meet someone here. We think he was sitting behind the wheel waiting and the killer drove up, got out of his car, walked alongside, leaned in the lowered window, and fired twice."

"How do you figure that?"

Instead of answering directly, Larkin took something from his jacket pocket. When he opened his hand Maxwell saw the little automatic against the paler skin of the palm. As he stared at it, Larkin added two empty shells.

"We found these on the floor in the back. The gun ejects from the right. When our man finished, he threw it on the seat beside Carr."

"Empty?"

"One left. Apparently he had no further use for it . . . A .25 Colt, as we suspected. Tell me, Mr. Maxwell, have you ever seen it before?"

Maxwell's dark gaze remained fixed on the gun as he remembered again the little automatic Louise had so unexpectedly turned on him that night so long ago.

He said he might have, and Larkin, accepting the reply, drew him closer to the stretcher and the two white-coated attendants who stood by, waiting for some word from the Inspector before they lifted their burden into the van. Then, instead of pulling the blanket down to uncover the face as Maxwell had expected, Larkin lifted the other end to reveal the legs.

"When my men removed the body from the sedan," he said, "one of them noticed something odd about one leg— not the leg itself, but an object attached to it so that when the fabric was pulled taut along the thigh it made a noticeable lump. He thought it advisable to investigate."

He ran a finger inside the right leg, and Maxwell saw first the slit that had been made in the trousers and then the expanse of skin underneath. Six or eight inches above the knee there was a strange-looking patch quite different from the surrounding area. Perhaps an inch-and-a-half wide and twice as long, the skin was whiter here, quite hairless, with what looked like some sort of stickiness along the edges.

He straightened, more perplexed than ever, to see that
Larkin had again extended an open palm. In the center,
still attached to the piece of white adhesive tape that apparently had been stuck to the inside of the thigh, was the
Q-shaped diamond pin and the emerald ring.

"Well, I'll be damned," he said wearily, aware of the in-
adequacy of his words but unable to think of anything
better.

"Quite," Larkin said. "And very ingenious. Any routine
search of his clothing we might have made would have revealed nothing unless we could have persuaded him to
strip . . . He took more of a chance with this," he added,
and produced a folded book of traveler's checks. "Thirty-
three hundred dollars."

He put the checks and jewels back into his jacket pocket
and for the first time sounded somewhat discouraged.

"Very confusing, wouldn't you say, Mr. Maxwell? And it
poses an interesting question. Did Carr take these things
after the murder, or did the killer take them, not knowing
he had been observed until Carr approached him at some
later time with the promise of silence in exchange for the
jewelry?"

"Why would the killer take them at all?"

"Possibly, as I said before, to confuse the issue and present the alternative of robbery as a motive. Had we found
the missing evidence on him earlier we would have arrested
him at once. In fact, he must have known that he would
have had a most difficult time proving his innocence."

Maxwell thought he heard an uncharacteristic sigh before
Larkin continued, "But it seems your candidate for the
murder of your wife has himself become a victim."

"Which makes it even tougher for you now," Maxwell
said.

Larkin chose to ignore the wry comment. "He must have
seen the killer last night, wouldn't you say? But what could
he expect to gain by his silence?"

It sounded like a rhetorical question, but Maxwell answered it anyway.

"I can think of two reasons."

"Oh?"

"One, if he took the jewelry and checks and then put the finger on the killer you would still continue looking for the missing loot and Carr would have a harder time getting off the island with it. To a guy like him forty thousand bucks in jewels would be pretty tempting."

"And two?"

"Blackmail. A chance to cash in even more. The only rub there is, who would have enough dough to make the risk worthwhile?" He stopped as a new and startling thought erupted. "You had men questioning the help at the inn. What did you find out about Sam Blake and that guy Russo?"

"They were seen to leave the dining room together. They did not come back. They stated they retired to their respective bungalows. With their secretaries," he added dryly, "who corroborate their statements."

Maxwell was not yet ready to give up on the idea. "They were on the opposite side of the inn from my wife, but it would have been a cinch to slip down to the cove and along the beach and up the other path."

"Unfortunately we can't prove it." Larkin watched the ambulance drive off and then stood by as a tow truck backed down the alley to be hooked up to Carr's sedan. Again he touched Maxwell's arm. "Let's sit here for a bit."

He stepped aside to speak to one of his men and Maxwell recognized the lanky figure of Sergeant Beaman; then Larkin was opening the door of his official sedan and motioning Maxwell ahead of him. He climbed in beside him but waited until Beaman took the front seat and turned on the dome light.

"I'm sure you see how the facts of tonight's homicide can be made to fit you, Mr. Maxwell."

Maxwell watched the Sergeant open a notebook and knew what was coming. "And anything I say, et cetera, et cetera, is that it?" he said resentfully.

"I'm afraid so. You see, we have one other bit of information that can be added to your present motives."

"Like what?"

"We were fortunate in getting in touch with one of the partners in the law firm you said handled your wife's affairs. Do you happen to know the terms of her will?"

"No."

"You were not aware that you are mentioned in it?"

"Hell, no."

"A bequest of one hundred thousand dollars."

"I don't believe it!" Maxwell snapped in that first instant of surprise. Then, realizing how that sounded, amended the statement: "I don't mean I think you made it up; it's just that—I mean—I don't know—" He finished feebly and tried again, still shaken by the unexpected knowledge but determined to make Larkin believe him.

"She could have done it, I guess. She was certainly generous enough the short time we were engaged. A hundred thousand would have been peanuts to her, anyway. It was probably just a whim—"

"Do you recall the date you were married?"

"Certainly," Maxwell said, and named it.

"Umm—yes. This codicil was added five days before. Although I find it strange that she did not take the trouble to cancel the bequest if she felt as bitter about your abandonment as you have led us to believe."

"Maybe she forgot it," Maxwell said, even as he knew such a response was inadequate. "To her it would hardly be enough to bother with."

"Or perhaps she still expected to get you back."

"It's possible," Maxwell said, not believing it. "She sure as hell didn't give up easily."

"In any event, you now have another reason to prove your innocence," Larkin said with some ambiguity.

This guy is baiting me, Maxwell thought with sudden clarity, and found the idea mildly astonishing. *He's leading up to something. Not just the lousy inheritance, but something more.*

"I don't need another reason, Inspector," he said in a show of temper. "I've got more damn reasons than I need already."

Again Larkin ignored the outburst. "I was referring to the law that exists in many of your states to the effect that a murderer cannot profit by his act."

Maxwell grunted irritably. "Sure. If I killed her I won't get the hundred grand unless I get away with it. Which means I have to be convicted first."

"Quite true."

Larkin removed his hat and brushed the rim absently. In the half-light his dark eyes were pinpoints of obscurity beneath the strong brows, and he seemed to be studying the motionless back of Sergeant Beaman.

Close by, there was the sound of a motor accelerating and Maxwell watched the tow truck start to roll off with Carr's sedan, two wheels of which had been winched clear of the paving. The silence came again and Larkin let it build—deliberately, it seemed.

It was then that Maxwell began to wonder if it was time to tell the Inspector about the attempted poisoning that morning. *If* indeed it had been poison in that bottle. It had tasted bitter, yes. But suppose it was quinine or something like that, put there as a warning of some kind, or perhaps a red herring. And even if Dr. Singh was able to isolate a poison, would Larkin accept his story?

In the first place, there was no witness of any kind. The fact that there was poison in the bottle would not eliminate the possibility that he, Maxwell, had put it there himself to allay suspicion, to turn the investigation into other channels.

No matter what he said, it would be pointed out that he was still alive. His story of how he had come to take only the tiniest sip of the concoction instead of a more normal swallow or two was something that could have been contrived . . .

So forget it, Maxwell! he told himself, and then Larkin was speaking again.

"We won't keep you much longer, Mr. Maxwell," he said. "Just tell us where you were and what you did from say, five o'clock this evening on. And this is for the record."

"I was at the Pelican sometime around five. The cook there prepares roasts and things I take with me on charters. I still hope to take Blake and his party to Bastique Monday and I wanted the ketch ready by noon . . . At five-thirty I had a date there with Valerie Atherton. We sat on the veranda and had a drink and did some talking.

"I don't know how long she stayed, but afterwards I went into the downstairs bar, had a couple more belts and something to eat. I don't know how long I was there either. When I was ready I went back to the Casurina. I was still sitting up when your man came."

He spoke forthrightly and without hesitation even though he knew a careful investigation might turn up a gap in time that could be questioned. There was always a chance his return to his room had not been noted.

"Not much of an alibi, is it?" he added casually. "While Carr is getting himself killed I'm sitting all by myself sucking on some sugarcane brandy."

"Did you see anyone when you returned to the Casurina?"

"There was nobody around downstairs, but one of the servants may have seen me park my car."

Larkin nodded and put his hat back on. He said, "Well—" letting the word drag, and right then Maxwell had a brainstorm.

He never knew what prompted it. It may have sprung from the feeling that he had lied enough—about his discovery of the body, about the poisoning attempt, about his movements that evening—or some perverse desire to prove his credibility; whatever the reason, he heard himself saying:

"Are you going to take a look at Carr's room?"

"As soon as I've arranged for someone to drive you home."

"Can I go with you?"

That got a reaction. Even in the car's poorly lighted interior he knew Larkin was watching him closely as he considered the request. Finally he said:

"Just curiosity, Mr. Maxwell? Or have you something more definite in mind?"

Maxwell said what he had in mind was not only definite but specific.

THE PELICAN HOTEL WAS very quiet as Sergeant Beaman took the proper key from behind the small desk. A happy and contented snoring came from behind one door as they went along the hall, but otherwise there was nothing to hear but the in-step tread of their shoes on the thin carpeting.

Once inside, Maxwell pulled a chair off to one side and watched the performance. Larkin had said, "Take the closet, Sergeant," and after that they conducted the search in silence. Beaman, having finished his chore long before his superior, went over to the desk where Larkin was going through the carbons sheet by sheet just as Maxwell had done.

From time to time he made a note. He examined the cameras to see if they contained any film. He took pains with the equipment case and Maxwell sat there smoking, approving of Larkin's well-tailored blue suit and shiny black oxfords, the white shirt, and the conservative maroon tie which seemed to match his eyes. When Larkin had finished he turned, head tipping slightly as he leaned his hips against the table desk and crossed his ankles.

"Well, Mr. Maxwell?" he said when he had finished his appraisal.

Maxwell stood up. He found the tiny bullet hole in the wood paneling at once and put a fingernail on the edge. Larkin exchanged glances with Beaman, studied Maxwell unhurriedly. When he was ready he pushed away from the desk and took a close hard look at the hole.

"What about it, Mr. Maxwell? Do you know what made it?"

"A bullet."

If he had any reaction, Larkin kept it well hidden. He examined the hole with a fingertip, nodded to Beaman. "Try your knife, Sergeant. Don't scratch it." He studied Maxwell again, his gaze speculative, the round ebony face revealing nothing.

"All right. How did you know it was there?"

Maxwell inspected the tip of his cigarette and took time to put his thoughts in order. He had to protect Marvin, but he saw that that was no problem, and now he began to speak, starting with his suspicions, already stated, about Leon Carr.

"That missing jewelry bothered me. Carr seemed the most likely candidate to take the two best pieces—if he had been there—and hope they wouldn't be missed.

"I told Miss Atherton I was going to pay Carr a visit. I guess I was a little desperate to find something useful that would take some of the pressure off me. The point is I came. When no one answered the door I stepped inside," he said and went on to explain why he had not turned on the overhead light and how he had stumbled over the typewriter case just as he heard the shot.

He was out of breath when he finished, watching Larkin every moment and trying to guess how he was accepting the story. He should have expected the question that followed. It came in such an offhand casual way that he had to regroup his thoughts quickly and proceed with care.

"Most interesting, Mr. Maxwell. But I've been wondering how you were able to enter the room in the first place. Is it the custom, I wonder, for the guests to leave their rooms unlocked?"

Maxwell hoped he was able to hide his momentary confusion. He had practically admitted illegal entry, but to make a direct statement to that effect with a man like Larkin could prove embarrassing. He did his best to brazen it out.

"I don't know about the other guests. I knocked and when there was no answer I tried the door and—"

He stopped abruptly, recalling how the Sergeant had taken the room key from the rack when they had come upstairs. Shaken by the obvious hole in his story, he hurried on, stubborn now and improvising as best he could.

"As a matter of fact, the key was right there in the lock. So"—he shrugged—"I turned it and went in."

"I see." Larkin's tone suggested nothing of the kind, but he would have made a good poker player, his expression changing hardly at all as he added, "And then when you left you locked the door behind you and put the key back in the rack behind the desk."

"Well—yes," Maxwell said, certain that the Inspector believed none of this and instantly grateful when Beaman came back from his probing and offered the little slug he had extracted from the wall.

Larkin rolled it between thumb and forefinger, glanced up again, his narrowed gaze impossible to diagnose before he nodded and dropped the subject.

"Our ballistic facilities here are limited, but sufficient, I think, to establish a reasonable comparison between this and the bullet removed from your wife. Dr. Singh should be able to provide another specimen from his autopsy on Mr. Carr . . .

"So our man was waiting on the rooftop"—he pointed to

the side window—"and he took his shot and missed. And what was your reaction when you were safe on the floor? I don't mean in the sense that you were no doubt outraged and quite possibly scared—"

"I know what you mean," Maxwell said. "I figured at first that the guy had followed me here. He tried to frame me by dumping my wife's body on the ketch"—again he dismissed the thought of mentioning the poisoned liquor—"and I assumed he thought I knew something that might put the finger on him."

"And you were satisfied with that theory?"

"Not when I'd had a chance to think. I decided he'd been waiting for Carr and pulled the trigger before he realized his mistake. What happened to Carr sort of proves it."

"I agree. Our man was certainly persistent."

Larkin's tone was casual enough, but something in his attitude still bothered Maxwell. He wasn't sure why but he was at once aware of an air of skepticism on Larkin's part. When that impression persisted, he said:

"I don't get it, Inspector."

This time some surprise showed. "Don't get what, Mr. Maxwell?"

"Somehow I get the idea that you think I'm making this up." He was sounding sullen now but he couldn't help it. "Maybe you think I put my wife's body on the ketch just to throw you off."

Larkin allowed himself a shrug. "In this business you try to consider all aspects of a case when it follows an unfamiliar pattern. A clever man might reason exactly as you have outlined it. If I may be hypothetical consider this:

"You kill your wife last night, with or without premeditation. You will admit the motives existed. To phone the police would be to establish almost exactly the time of death, for which you have no alibi. You are aware there are others with motives, that your wife has the capacity to invite violence. You say, 'All right. If no one discovers the murder I'll come back and put her on my ketch'—and remember you have the small boat handy to do the job—'and in the morning my mate will discover her, and no one in his right mind will think I would deliberately involve myself so directly.'"

He paused to see how Maxwell was following his reasoning. "You must admit the possibility, Mr. Maxwell. The idea was to confuse us and the issue, and I will admit it has. I'd say you were an intelligent man. I haven't decided yet just how clever you are, but if my hypothesis has merit, I'd say we have a similar situation here, wouldn't you agree?

"You kill your wife, and then you find out that somehow Mr. Carr knows it. Since we know now *he* didn't kill her, he assumes it's safe to take the ring and pin when he discovers her body. He puts pressure on you, or perhaps he makes an agreement to remain silent so long as he can get away with, say, forty thousand dollars' worth of jewelry. But you're afraid of him. You can't trust him. You decide he has to go. *You* go to that roof with that little gun you already have—"

He shook his head, dissatisfied, it seemed, with this hypothesis: "A much simpler and just as effective way would be to come here, stand back, fire the slug into the wall for us to find. Because you have already made your date with Mr. Carr for later in the evening, prepared to kill him. You do so, go to your room, and wait for us to pick you up. You tell your story and at the proper time find a way to bring us here and show us a bullet hole to convince us that someone intent on killing Mr. Carr had put it there."

He smiled again, white teeth showing, and made an offhand gesture before adding, "As I said, this is all hypothesis; but a tenable one, I think. What do *you* think of it?"

Maxwell had to take a few seconds to reply, because he wasn't sure just what he did think. Such reasoning impressed him, and he had listened not only with growing amazement but with the uncomfortable feeling that he had not improved his position in the slightest. He felt badgered and buffeted, and to make sure none of this showed, he laughed derisively.

"If I were home and an American detective threw that at me, I'd say it was a lot of crap," he said, and found his tone of voice distasteful. "But since you've treated me with consideration so far, I'll be honest and admit you have a point."

Larkin brushed the admission aside. "It's simply that we do things differently under our system, Mr. Maxwell. We make no charges or arrests—unless we think a suspect may try to run—until we have cause. When we do, we usually manage to get a conviction."

He adjusted the brim of his hat and nodded to Beaman. "But I think we have finished here for tonight. Unless we find something more conclusive, your formal statement can wait until Monday."

"I have an important charter starting around Monday noon," Maxwell said, wanting to get this part over with.

"So I understand. Mr. Blake and friends."

"You have the authority to keep me on the island?"

"With cause."

"Well, damn it!" Maxwell growled with mounting exasperation. "Do you have it or don't you?"

"Not yet, Mr. Maxwell. Not yet."

Another nod and Sergeant Beaman opened the door and stood aside. Larkin made a polite after-you gesture and waited for Maxwell to lead the way.

18

ON SUNDAY MORNING Alan Maxwell slept later than he had for months. The habit of early morning rising when on board the *Annabel* normally carried over on his mornings ashore, even when he had a hangover. Now it was the sound of the maid unlocking his door that brought him awake, and he opened one eye as she giggled and excused herself. When she started to withdraw, he told her to wait.

He was trying to get his brain in gear and at the same time make some sort of plan for the day. This he found difficult, because all he could think of at first was what had happened to him the previous day. He took time to form a quick mental pattern from the time Oscar Jones had hammered on his door in the early morning right up to the moment he had climbed into bed. By then it had been after one, and his sense of exhaustion and depression had overcome any desire for a drink. The last thing he recalled was winding his watch.

"Could you bring me some breakfast, Ernestina—or is it Olive?"

"Oh, yes sir." She did not bother to correct him. "You like eggs, bacon?"

"Crisp. You know, lots of cooking. A piece of melon.

Toast—a slice of that penny-bread—and bring lots of coffee. Okay?" . . .

He threw off the sheets and stood up. He stretched, yawned, scratched his head and then his chest hair. He considered a shower, but decided to postpone it until after he'd had a dip. He grabbed his shaving things and wrapped a towel around his middle before peeking into the hall to make sure the bathroom was unoccupied.

The breakfast did wonders for him, both physically and mentally. He ate naked, and when he had finished the last of his coffee he put on swimtrunks, aware that for some strange reason his morale was surprisingly high. He took his cigarettes and lighter, locked his wallet in his little liquor cabinet, and went downstairs.

A couple, apparently guests of the Casurina, were standing at the end of the small jetty surveying Young's Island, and he picked his way along the narrow ribbon of dark sand between the water's edge and the wire fences protecting the four bungalows, half-hidden by roof-high shrubbery, that separated the Casurina from the Aquatic Club.

There were only a few customers at the club at this hour, but there would be others later, after church, it being a custom for many members who had plantations upcountry to come in with their families and make a day of it.

Moving at once to a bench near the end of the pier, he left cigarettes, lighter, and watch with his towel and dived off the side closest to the *Annabel,* doing ten hard and well-executed crawl strokes before flipping over on his back for air. For a few seconds he considered swimming out to the ketch for a quick check, but then decided, *The hell with it for today.*

He was not sure how long he floated, thinking of nothing in particular, pleased with the quiet as he watched the sky and clouds. Some, he noted, were in the proper quadrant for a shower before too long. For it was characteristic of the weather pattern that one could usually tell which threatening clouds would bring rain and which meant nothing at all.

He was still daydreaming when he heard someone hail him, although the call came three times before he understood it was for him. When he turned over, he saw the two men near the end of the pier, and he thought the one who was waving was Albert Carswell.

He came out dripping and reaching for his towel, to find Sam Blake, looking very sharp in his off-white slacks and lightweight blue blazer, waiting with Carswell.

"They told us at your place you might be here. Can you sit up there on the porch like that so we can have a drink?"

"Sure." Maxwell toweled his head and wiped his face, at the same time wondering what had prompted the visit. "Bathing suits permitted . . . Good morning, Albert."

Carswell replied without enthusiasm, his washed-out blue eyes sad in his thin peanut-colored face. He wore his regulation white drill, a watch chain draped across his vest, and his bony, liver-spotted hands had a noticeable tremor.

"I stopped to see Mr. Blake," he said by way of explanation, "and he thought I might as well drive out with him."

Maxwell led the way to a corner of the veranda, waved them to chairs as he signaled for a waiter and draped the towel across his shoulders.

"I guess I tied one on last night," Blake said, "for no reason at all . . . I want a pink gin," he told the waiter, "and bring a bottle of Heineken with it."

Carswell ordered a Scotch-and-soda and Maxwell said he'd have a beer. Then Blake was talking, his voice direct and businesslike.

"I guess you know what happened to that guy Carr last night."

"I have an idea I was the first to know," Maxwell said dryly. "Larkin sent a car to pick me up at my place last night."

"Larkin? Yeah, the Inspector. He's a pretty smart cop."

"Have you seen him?"

"This morning. He and some sergeant were around before we were up. They waited while we dressed. Before he told us what it was all about he asked if I minded if he and his man looked the rooms over. I told him no."

"Did he give you any trouble?"

"Hah!" It was a dry humorless sound, and Blake waited while the drinks were served. "Me, no. Tony, yes. The sergeant found a gun in Tony's room. I didn't know he had the damn thing."

The news served only to confirm Maxwell's impression of Russo, and now he said, "Why the hell would he bring a gun all the way from Boston?"

"Habit, I guess."

"What is he, anyway? A hood? What's he doing with you? How does he fit in your development?"

Blake tossed off his pink gin and poured beer, intent on the head he was making.

"He's had some hotel experience in Vegas," he said. "Some of our people thought he might be useful when our inn starts operating. I didn't know him before this trip, and when we get home I'm going to recommend that he stay there. He'd be no good here; he's a city boy . . . But what I want to know about now is you."

"In what way?"

"Well, is Larkin going to let you take us to Bastique or not? You didn't kill Carr, did you? Can he hold you?"

"I don't think he will."

"Could you come up with an alibi for last night? I understand Carr got it sometime after ten."

Maxwell tasted his beer and watched the Young's Island launch discharge a load of guests. He had been wondering if it might have been possible for Russo to have killed Carr; he was also curious about Carswell since he could not forget the motive the older man had for getting his, Maxwell's, wife out of the way.

"No alibi," he said. "I was in my room sucking on some sugarcane brandy. What about you?"

"Me?" Blake leaned back, scowling and affronted it seemed, by the inference. "What the hell would I know about it?"

"Didn't Larkin ask you where you were last night?"

"And we told him. Having dinner and listening to that Saturday night offering the inn has. The band wasn't too great, but it was a lot easier on my ears than that steel thing. Some of those calypsos were pretty cute, I mean the way they can make them up. We did too much drinking and staggered off somewhere around midnight."

"Russo too?"

"Certainly . . . Look!" he sat up straight and shook an index finger at Maxwell. "If you think you can tie Tony into any of this, forget it."

Maxwell grinned and said, "Okay, Sam. But what about that gun?"

"That's why I phoned Albert this morning—to make sure we didn't get held up over that. Nothing to it. Wrong caliber, I guess. Larkin confiscated it, and maybe there'll be a slap-on-the-wrist fine for bringing it in."

Maxwell was only half-listening now as his thoughts moved on to focus on Carswell. The older man had already finished his Scotch and was revolving the glass absently in his long fingers as he looked fixedly out across the water. He came to with a start when Maxwell addressed him.

"What?" he said with some confusion. "I'm afraid I wasn't listening."

"I asked if you'd had an official visit this morning."

"Oh, yes. Naturally . . . I wonder if I might have another of these," he added, and beckoned to a waiter. "Yes, indeed. Sometime around nine, I'd say. Captain Andrews and another officer in plainclothes. Wanted me to account for my movements last night."

"Could you?"

"Oh, yes." He smiled ruefully. "Unfortunately, without the necessary corroboration. You see, I'd had an early meal at the club. I was at my place before eight and I did a bit of solitary drinking and indulged in various fantasies, most of them pleasant and all centering in some fashion around my commission and the future of Bastique."

Such forthrightness was disarming. Blake laughed loudly and Maxwell chuckled until a new thought came to sober him. For in those next seconds he was back on the *Annabel* when Carswell and Osborne came aboard yesterday morning and a drink was suggested.

Why, if Carswell was as innocent as he pretended, had he, who drank local rum, and Scotch when someone else was buying, asked for sugarcane brandy at that particular time?

The thought nagged him anew and he fought against making any ill-considered conclusion. It also reminded him that it was time to get in touch with Dr. Singh and find out how successful he had been in his tests. He heard Blake call for a check, watched him put a bill down, listened as he said:

"Well, the hell with Carr. He probably had it coming. He must have known who killed your wife—or thought he did —and made the mistake of trying to chisel a payment of some kind."

He pushed back his chair. "Let's go, Albert." He stood up and then, rudely ignoring the older man, turned to Maxwell. "Why don't you have some lunch with us at the inn? Russo's been sulking and I can't understand half of what the two chicks are saying." Without waiting for an acceptance but taking it for granted, he added, "How about one o'clock? We'll have a couple of drinks first."

Maxwell watched them go and then went inside, the towel draped over his shoulders, and strolled over to the bar telephone. He asked for a directory and called Dr. Singh's home number. The maid who answered after five rings had a broad native accent almost impossible to understand, but he finally translated the words to mean the doctor and family were at church and would be back some time after noon . . .

When Maxwell had showered and dressed he went out to the Consul and drove the half-mile to Oscar Jone's neat concrete-block house. A small boy and girl in their bright clean Sunday school clothes were playing with a puppy, and Maxwell asked if their father was home.

Oscar, apparently overhearing the request, appeared in the doorway, his arm around a plump, pretty girl some years younger than he, with a smooth round face and a complexion two shades darker.

She gave him a shy good morning, and Oscar said, "Everything all right, Mr. Max. We go tomorrow?"

"It looks that way—if my luck holds."

"You order the meat and things?"

Maxwell nodded and said Oscar should be aboard fairly early. "You know what to do, and when I come along we'll take her down to the town dock and get the supplies aboard. If things work out, we can shove off early in the afternoon."

"Who does Mr. Blake have this time?"

"A fellow named Russo who doesn't say much, and two girls."

Oscar's eyes showed a lot of white and he started to grin, glanced at his wife, and withheld comment.

"Things'll be ready when you are," he said.

19

It was after three when Alan Maxwell pulled up in front of Dr. Singh's home and knocked at the door. He had telephoned again from the lobby of the Villa Inn, and this time had talked to the doctor. The news had been something less than satisfying.

"I ran some tests," Singh had said. "I told you there was no cyanide in the bottle. Neither was there any arsenic, nicotine, or strychnine or any compound thereof which might be used in insecticides or rat poison. Frankly, I'm not sure I can do much more, unless we mail a sample to Port of Spain or Barbados."

Maxwell had accepted the results as gracefully as he could, and then, because he hated to let go, he remembered the medical volume Singh had shown him the day before.

"Will you be in after lunch?" he had asked.

"I'm afraid not for a while. We're planning to take the children for a ride up the coast this afternoon. Of course, a doctor can't be absent for very long"—a small chuckle accompanied this—"so I should be back by five."

"Well, look," Maxwell had said, unhappy about waiting that long. "There will be a maid at your place, won't there?"

"Oh, yes."

"Could you leave word with her to let me in? If it's not an imposition, I'd like to spend some time with that book on legal medicine you mentioned. You also have one of those pharmacology volumes that lists and describes all the drugs like an encyclopedia, don't you?"

"I have."

"If you left those two in your reception room, I could just sit there and go through them. I'll take good care of them."

There were some anxious seconds of silence before permission was given, somewhat reluctantly it seemed.

"You perhaps have some thoughts of your own about the substance in the bottle?"

"None. I know it will probably be a waste of time but it can't do any harm. Who knows? I might come up with some wild idea. You know, like a suggestion. At the least, I'll probably have some questions to put to you when you get back." He mentally crossed his fingers. "Or is that asking too much?"

"Not at all. I understand how you feel. Yes, I'll speak to the maid. She'll show you into the reception room and the books will be on the desk. I wish you luck, Mr. Maxwell."

Lunch at the Villa Inn with Blake and company had turned out rather more pleasantly than Maxwell had expected. He had found Sam Blake sitting alone at a round table back by the pool, with places set for five. His florid face was at ease, and he had a thoroughly relaxed look about him, a half-smoked cigar between his fingers, and the remains of a bloody mary in front of him.

"The others'll be here shortly," he said genially. "Sit down. What're you drinking?"

Maxwell took the chair next to Blake, considered the question. It had been some time since he'd had a bloody mary, so he said he'd have one of those and Blake gave the order. No reference was made then or later to murder or the police. Blake had seemed relaxed and preoccupied and Maxwell offered little on his own until he saw Russo and the two girls coming through the dining room.

He was not sure just what prompted his next remark but he realized as he heard his words that it was the first time he had ever attempted to kid Blake.

"Tell me," he said, "can you take those two off the company income tax as a business expense?"

For a moment as those hooded eyes inspected him he wondered if he had gone too far; then he saw the humorous lights that could not be disguised.

"Why not?" Blake grunted. "They're essential."

"If they can write a legible hand they're secretaries?"

"Exactly. The government doesn't have to know what kind of secretaries, and you're not the gabby sort, or all you'd ever be in this set-up is a charter-boat skipper . . . Sit down, girls."

Maxwell rose and the platinum-haired Elsie gave him a big hello and took the chair next to him. Agnes smiled and said, "Hello, Mr. Maxwell," and he said, "Alan," and she beamed and came back with "All right, Alan."

They ordered their gin-and-tonics and Russo, who had said nothing at all, asked for his usual rum punch. Both girls wore shorts and blouses. Their faces and arms and legs had begun to tan, and the amount of smooth young flesh displayed was a little hard to ignore.

They had chatted back and forth all through lunch and only one thing seemed important to them; they were dying, they said, to see the French liner that had piled up on a reef not far from Bastique.

"It's still there, isn't it?" Agnes asked, brushing her red hair out of one eye. "What's going to happen to it?"

"The company agents have been dickering with some salvage companies. It's no good for anything but scrap."

"Can we go aboard?"

"No. They have a couple of men there to keep what's left from being cannibalized. It's not much out of our way. We can sail around it. Did you bring a camera?"

"I did," Elsie said, and when he felt her hand lightly on his knee he tried not to look at her. "So did Tony, didn't you, Tony?"

Russo's stone-faced, blank-eyed grunt was vaguely affirmative. He offered little more to the conversation, ignoring Maxwell when he thanked Blake for the lunch and said good-bye to the girls.

The maid who opened the door of Dr. Singh's home had a fat, broad-nosed black face that wore a sad and mournful look. Her "Good evening" had a sullen undertone, as though she resented this intrusion on her privacy on a Sunday afternoon. She nodded when Maxwell gave his name, and waved him toward the door of the reception room.

"The doctor say the books are on the desk. You want I should close the door?"

Maxwell said it didn't matter. "I'll let you know when I leave," he added, and then forgot her.

The two volumes on the desk looked formidable and he considered them with some misgivings as he struggled with the nagging thought that this amateurish venture into toxicology was probably a lot of nonsense as well as a waste of time. Stubbornness alone made him lift the books one after another. Each was three or four inches thick and weighed at least four pounds.

The pharmacology book, which he examined first, not reading but simply flipping through it, was totally discouraging. For what he saw was page after page of drug names, most of them foreign to him, interspersed with color plates illustrating in exact size and shape the pills and capsules described in the text.

After a moment or two of aimless contemplation he tried the book on legal medicine and was somewhat encouraged to note that there were a lot of good photographs of wounds of all types as well as corpses in various positions of death, some of them downright gruesome.

"Okay, damn it," he said finally. "You asked for it."

The sound of his voice and some perverse sense of the absurd made him look round for a chair. He picked out the most comfortable-looking one and took the books with him.

He put the drug book on the floor and started on the other, aware now that the text and photographs had been divided into chapters dealing with specific causes of death: gunshot wounds, knifings, blunt instruments, rope burns, the results of certain types of auto accidents, the bloated, ugly, naked bodies of drowning victims.

The chapters on poisons were toward the end and consisted of text and diagrams—the latter, meaningless to him, as were the formulas whereby the experienced technician could test and determine the makeup and composition of specific poisons. Ignoring the diagrams, he took the poisons paragraph by paragraph, alphabetically, giving extra attention to those he had heard or read about.

Some were more fully explained than others, but in each case the symptoms were given, possible antidotes, the effects on whichever organs were involved, the signs to look for in an autopsy, the conclusions that could be made.

He went through every one listed, passing over the poisons that seemed unlikely for one reason or another. He finally eliminated all but two, rereading each word with care, channeling his imagination as possibilities presented themselves. In the end, he had hope where none had existed before, and the thought that he could be on the right track brought a stir of excitement as he put aside that volume and consulted the index of the pharmacology book. He found what he wanted without difficulty, his frown fixed and dark gaze intent as he absorbed each and every detail, not only for the basic drug but the various forms in which it could be administered.

He was still sitting with the open book in his lap, no longer aware of time or his surroundings, when he heard a tap at the door. He glanced up, startled, aware that the maid had spoken but too far away in his thoughts to understand what she wanted. He had to ask her to repeat herself, and she said:

"Would you like some tea, sir?"

Pleased somehow that he had finally been accepted as a bona fide guest, he stood up and thanked her. He put the books back on the desk, found a dollar bill, and tucked it into her palm, asking her to please thank the doctor and to tell him that he would telephone later.

20

A SHOWER HAD COME AND GONE while Maxwell had been busy with his books, but the late afternoon sun was out now, the shiny pavements already beginning to dry as he drove along the coast highway.

Sunday afternoon was the time for the islanders without cars to promenade along the side of the road. There weren't too many men, but the women and children in their bright frocks made a pleasing color scheme against the background of drab roadside houses and shacks, the four corners of some supported by hunks of coral. The donkey carts were missing, but the bicycles were out in force, and driving took some skill until Maxwell approached the plateau on which stood Hardin Hall.

The flagged court with its swimming pool was on the right and partly behind that wing, and as he stopped in the parking area he saw both the Osborne car and Albert Carswell's old Morris. Valerie Atherton must have been looking for him, because as he moved round the corner of the wing she stood up and came to meet him.

She had a smile for him and he was impressed again by the lovely way she moved. The copper-colored hair had the familiar windblown casualness, and he thought he saw approval in the green eyes when she took his hand and squeezed it once.

"Am I late?"

"No." She shook her head. "The others only just came. What have *you* been up to all day?"

He told her he had got up late and had a swim. He spoke of seeing Blake and Carswell at the Aquatic Club, and the luncheon invitation that followed.

"For the last hour or more I've been doing a little research."

"Oh?" The brows arched prettily. "Can you tell me about it?"

"Yes, but I'd like the others to hear my theory . . . I guess you know about Leon Carr."

"Oh, yes." She shrugged faintly and made a face. "Bright and early. Captain Andrews in his Sunday suit. Just routine, he said, but he still wanted to know who was where last night. I suppose if the four of us hadn't played bridge until quite late we'd all be under suspicion. What about you?"

Maxwell told her as he counted the roll. An awning sloped down from one wall of the house to give protection, if such was needed, to a long linen-covered table with a tea service and drinks and plates of small sandwiches and cookies and a chocolate cake.

A short black man in a white jacket presided behind the table, and a young and pretty maid with smooth sepia skin stood by to provide service when needed. It pleased him some to see that Michael and Wanda were sitting side by side at the far end of the pool, their backs to the house. Carswell and Osborne sat informally on either side of, but not close to Dorothy Atherton.

Valerie had slipped her arm through his as they moved slowly toward the others, and now he gave a nod at the far end of the pool.

"How's Michael?"

"Subdued but convalescing nicely."

"Your mother's persistent methods worked out okay then?"

"They usually do somehow. He resented all of us at first last night, especially her for insisting that he stay home for dinner. But he's too well mannered to sulk in public, and the bridge game helped. And Wanda—"

She gave his arm a squeeze, sounding so pleased that the words bubbled out.

"I mean, she was wonderful, really. I don't think I ever appreciated her before. Very poised but not stuffy, with a sort of casual dignity. Naturally no one mentioned your wife, and Wanda treated Michael just as she treated us, not catering to him in the slightest but very adult about the whole thing.

"Then when she came this afternoon Michael seemed actually glad to see her. His eyes lit up a little I think, and it was his idea that they go off by themselves. I guess I never realized what a terrific person she is and Michael is an idiot if he doesn't snap out of it and marry her . . . Furthermore," she added with some spirit, "I intend to tell him so before I go back to Barbados."

"Tomorrow?" he asked, warmed somehow by her evaluation and conviction about Wanda Osborne.

"The afternoon flight. I have to be here in the morning to sign away my rights to Bastique, I suppose—"

She checked herself, seeing that the others had looked up, and terminated the conversation. Now Maxwell continued to Dorothy Atherton, gave a small formal bow, and accepted the offered hand.

He said, "Good afternoon, Mrs. Atherton," and she said, "Good afternoon, Alan. Sit down and let Grace get you some tea."

He glanced at Carswell as he found a chaise and Valerie sat down beside him: the same white drill suit and slicked-down mousy hair, balancing a cup of tea and two finger sandwiches on his knee and looking unhappy about it. For they all knew that one cup of tea was mandatory on these Sunday afternoons. You could have all the drinks you wanted afterward, but that first cup was protocol.

The maid brought a tray with tea for Valerie and Maxwell and a small plate of sandwiches and tiny cakes. He could also feel Valerie nudge him, and it was hard to keep a straight face. George Osborne had said nothing at all. He had put his tea aside, and now he handed it to the maid and stood up. He had a cane leaning against the back of his chair, but he ignored it as he limped once and then straightened and stepped to the table to order a drink. He wore an old but very good-looking suit of white tropical worsted, and this reminded Maxwell of one he had ordered when he had first come to the islands—only to find that the trousers were a little too good-looking to be practical.

The jacket, lined, was great; but the trousers were so close to being sheer that he found his undershorts showed. If they were colored you could identify the color; white ones were one's best bet, but even then you could tell where they ended. Now he noticed that the bottom edges of Osborne's shorts were uneven, as though the seat had caught in his crotch somehow and he was too embarrassed to shake it down in front of the others.

Maxwell swallowed some tea and ate a sandwich, not looking at anyone but trying to arrange his thoughts in the proper sequence, to find the necessary determination to get on with what he knew had to be done. He was worried about what Valerie would think of him and how she would react; but he also knew it was a chance he had to take because there was no other way. He took a small breath and looked at Dorothy Atherton, admiring again the strong handsome face, the well-groomed gray-white hair, and almost-unlined features.

"Val tells me you had another brief visit from the police this morning."

She lowered her cup and eyed him coolly—displeased, it seemed, that he should even mention the subject.

"A Captain Andrews. Inquired about our whereabouts last evening. Fortunately we were all here . . . I heard something about that Mr. Carr," she said tightly. "I believe he worked for your late wife. She seems to have spread her contamination even after her death."

"Inspector Larkin sent for me," Maxwell said, and explained what had happened and what he had learned. "I didn't have an alibi, and I don't know whether Larkin believed me or not . . . Do you think he believed you, Albert?"

Carswell put his cup and saucer aside and wet his lips. "I can only hope so. Since my maid does not live in, there was no way I could prove I stayed home last evening."

"George?"

Osborne, who was obviously in one of his grumpier moods, gave Maxwell a long look, the deepset gray eyes resentful.

"Same as Albert," he said finally. "Wanda fixed a salad for me before she left for here. I had a few drinks and was in bed before she got home."

Maxwell only half-heard this reply, for the pattern that had begun to form in his brain seemed almost complete. The discovery he had made from his research in Dr. Singh's books had served to weld his bits and pieces of information into a hopeful hypothesis, but he had to be sure about the one missing piece of his puzzle before he dared to make an accusation. He stood up, ready now to take his gamble.

"May I use your phone?" He looked at Dorothy Atherton, aware that there was an extension under the awning. Her surprise showed, but she waved toward the table, and he said, "I'd prefer—I mean, if you don't mind—"

She knew what he meant, and her strong brows arched

with disapproval. "Of course, if it's a personal call—" She let it go at that. "By all means. I'm sure you know where it is."

He left as quickly as he could, gaze straight ahead. The telephone he wanted was in the main hall. He got Police Headquarters without delay, but then bogged down temporarily. The sergeant on duty informed him that the Inspector was not in; neither was Captain Andrews or Sergeant Beaman. He had some difficulty obtaining Larkin's home number; but he threatened and bluffed as much as he dared and in the end the duty sergeant weakened.

He thought it was a maid who answered at the Larkin residence and he had a bit of trouble making himself understood. After what seemed like five minutes the Inspector at last came on the line. Maxwell asked one direct question, and when he had his answer he came to the point.

"I'm at Hardin Hall, Inspector. I think you ought to come out here some time soon. Are you free now?"

"We're having our tea, Mr. Maxwell. I suppose I could leave in another fifteen or twenty minutes . . . Hardin Hall? I'm not sure Mrs. Atherton would approve."

"It wouldn't be a social call, Inspector."

The "Ohh—" that followed was full of doubt, and Maxwell thought he could detect a sigh of weariness or resignation. "You have some additional evidence I should know about?"

"I'm pretty sure I can do better than that. Finish your tea, but think it over. My hunch says it will be worth a trip."

He hung up to forestall further argument or explanation and when he went back to the terrace everyone watched him with wariness or suspicion. He sat down next to Valerie again but took pains to avoid her eyes.

"I just called Inspector Larkin," he said, deciding he might as well get it over with. He got the reaction he expected from Mrs. Atherton. A muscle rippled in the angle of her jaw as her mouth tightened.

"You're not suggesting you invited him here."

"I'm afraid I did."

"Indeed. Your presumptuousness appalls me, Mr. Maxwell."

"I'm quite aware of that."

"May I ask why?"

"Because this is where he's going to find the person who murdered my wife and Leon Carr; and who tried twice, possibly once by mistake, to kill me."

He was acutely conscious of the reaction that followed. Carswell's bony jaw sagged as his mouth opened silently. Osborne's glare was more intent, and the quick small gasp that came from Valerie bothered him. The only spoken response came, as he had expected, from his hostess.

"You're serious, aren't you?" she said, with mounting incredulity.

"Quite serious, Mrs. Atherton."

"You can't mean all of us are under suspicion. Valerie, for instance; or Wanda; or Michael—"

He ignored the sarcasm and kept his voice even and controlled. "Michael could have killed my wife. He admits they quarreled bitterly. Knowing her as I did, I can understand how she might have goaded him to violence and grabbed the little gun she had, how she could have been shot when, to protect himself, he managed to turn the muzzle her way."

He put his hand up impatiently to block off a reply. "But since I'm sure the one who killed my wife also killed Carr, and since there are three witnesses that Michael was here all evening he's in the clear, along with Valerie and Wanda."

"Am I to take it I was also in contention, Mr. Maxwell?"

"You were until last night. You are a very strong character, physically, mentally, morally. You had the same motive for wanting my wife out of the way that George had. It wasn't the Bastique deal as such with you; it was your son and George's daughter. You had worked it out, the two of you, and it was the thing you wanted most, their marriage.

"It was practically as good as done until my wife comes along and in five days has your son wrapped around her little finger. Yes, Mrs. Atherton, you had a motive. Your son's happiness and future had to be protected at any cost, and frankly I doubt if you'd stop at murder." He shrugged and took a small breath. "Fortunately the bridge game eliminates you unless two people were involved, which is not exactly impossible."

He waited for her reply but it was Carswell clearing his throat that broke the silence.

"Just one damn minute, Alan!" he sputtered indignantly. "It seems to me you've just eliminated everyone but George and me, and of course yourself."

"On the nose, Albert. No alibi for either murder—you weren't at the table Friday night *all* of the time, remember —and as for motive, let's check it out and see how it sounds. Or do I have to go into detail about your dream of selling Bastique, the money and time and effort you spent finding a buyer? And finally it's not a dream anymore. You have the buyer. The sale is simply a formality. Five percent of $370,000 plus additional commissions when the development starts to expand.

"Right, Albert?" he said. "And like that, it's all gone. Because a woman with money comes down here to see how many ways she can hurt me. By buying Bastique and leaving it undeveloped, my chance to re-establish myself vanishes—but so does yours. Even if Blake's crowd met her price, so long as she had Michael on her side, with his equalizing proxy, she could force the matter into the courts for God knows how long."

Before Carswell could answer, and by the crushed and hopeless expression on his face, he had none, Dorothy

Atherton showed another side of herself that Maxwell could not help but admire.

"*Michael!*" The summons was polite but peremptory, and got an immediate response.

Her son—sitting close beside Wanda, at the far end of the pool—rose, tall and blond and handsome in his light-gray slacks and blue blazer.

"Bring Wanda along."

They came together, exchanging shy sidelong glances. Maxwell, watching the older woman, saw her smile, and the blue eyes, so often imperious, now held a fond approving look.

"I wish you'd run an errand for me, please," she said. "I've been meaning to mention it before but somehow it slipped my mind. You see, I'm afraid I left a scarf at the Villa Inn Friday night, and I'd like you to run down there now and have a word with the manager. It's a Liberty pattern, mostly red with some dark-green background. I'm sure Wanda wouldn't mind."

Michael had difficulty concealing his momentary impatience. He hesitated, the quick frown showing. But the habit of unprotesting obedience remained strong, and the girl helped.

"Mind?" she said brightly. "I'd love to go. It's the nicest part of the day for a ride." She touched his arm. "I'll even drive, if you like."

Her quick enthusiasm brought a smile from the man, and his mother said, "An offer like that deserves a drink while you're there, don't you think, Michael? We'll still be here when you get back."

They left in silence, arm in arm, and as they disappeared round the corner, Valerie spoke to her mother, her voice quietly approving.

"You have no such scarf, Mother, and you know it."

"Neither could I see any reason for them to be a witness to Mr. Maxwell's absurdities . . . Well," she added coldly, her gaze bright and intent, "now that we all have motives, you might as well get on with your accusations."

Maxwell thought it over, wanting to look at Valerie, to touch her, to make her understand this was something he had to do.

"You know that someone killed my wife in her bungalow Friday, probably while we all were at the inn, and then, for some reason, moved the body to my boat. I don't know why, but as a guess I'd say it was to involve me as much as possible and at the same time confuse the police and hinder their investigation.

"What you don't know is that someone, obviously the killer, took a shot at me last night shortly after eight o'clock. I think now, and so does Inspector Larkin, that this was a case of mistaken identity, and fortunately for me the guy missed."

He went on quickly to re-create the scene and explain his reasons for wanting to have a thorough look at Leon Carr's room. He told about the inventory the police had made of his wife's room and the missing ring, pin, and traveler's checks.

"Carr seemed like the logical person to do a thing like that if he had a chance, and we know now that this is just what happened. The fact that he's dead is proof enough that he also must have known who shot my wife—don't ask me how. He took the most valuable pieces he could find, and they were found on his body last night," he said and he described how they had been taped to one thigh. "He also made the mistake of holding out on the police."

He kept talking, wanting to make them understand how he felt when he heard the shot, to be sure they could visualize the awkward stumble and loss of balance that probably saved his life.

"All right," he said when no one tried to interrupt. "I'll go along with the Inspector's theory. He thinks whoever had the gun—and from the type of wounds in Carr and my wife and an estimate of the caliber of the bullet, it's probably the same gun—thought I was Carr when I turned the light on in Carr's room, and took his shot at me. Somehow he must have met Carr later and finished the job.

"But here's something Larkin doesn't know, and neither does anyone else except the person who deliberately tried to kill me yesterday morning."

He heard Valerie say, "*Alan!*" in a hushed and horrified whisper. Carswell was staring at him, bewilderment and consternation in the wide-open blue eyes. Dorothy Atherton's frown and steady gaze seemed more skeptical than startled; Osborne's reply carried an undertone of contempt.

"Tried to kill you," he said. "When yesterday morning? You looked all right when Albert and I were aboard."

"*How*, Alan?" Carswell said, his voice husky as he phrased the question.

Maxwell studied the narrow, slack-skinned face, examined the eyes again. They seemed to reflect some inner emotional disturbance but remained unwavering as he waited for a reply.

Still a bit unsure of the proper approach, Maxwell began obliquely.

"Let me ask you a question, Albert. When you came aboard the *Annabel* you said a drink might be in order, specifically sugarcane brandy. Do you remember?"

"Yes, I do, now that you mention it."

"For any particular reason or was it just coincidence?"

"Coincidence?" This time the eyes blinked. "I—I'm afraid I don't understand. I mean, we all know you're rather partial to—"

"But you're not."

"Quite the contrary," Carswell said reprovingly. "I seldom drink it because I can rarely afford it. The local rum does well enough for my daily rum cocktails and swizzles. In the old days when the planters in the country had no ice they'd sit on the veranda with a bottle of rum, a pitcher of water, and a bottle of Angostura and be quite content. Even today I take more or less the same view. However, when someone else picks up the tab," he added honestly, "I usually order whisky. But as I say, knowing your fondness—"

He paused, and his face began to bunch around the eyes. "But why all the fuss about sugarcane brandy, Alan? Does it have some significance?"

"I began to think so," Maxwell said, and again he was talking in quick concise sentences, leaning forward now and trying not to overemphasize the points he was hoping to make.

His imagination helped as he re-created the scene in the cabin of the *Annabel* when he had made his drink of brandy and soda. He tried to paint a mental picture of the glass which had been too full, and the small stooping sip he had taken to avoid spilling the drink. He described the bitter taste, the bewilderment and shock of understanding that had followed when the impact of his discovery became clear.

"What you're saying," Dorothy Atherton said in flat unemotional tones, "is that someone came aboard your boat earlier that morning and poisoned that bottle."

"I am."

"Choosing the sugarcane brandy because you were unlikely to offer it to anyone else?"

"Right."

"Later Albert and George came out and Albert suggested a drink of brandy. What did you tell him?"

"I said I was all out."

"What did you do with the bottle?"

"I took it to Dr. Singh to see if he could identify the poison."

"You didn't go to the police? . . . Why not?"

Maxwell sighed. His throat was getting dry and he felt

a moment of discouragement when he realized how far he still had to go.

"Because so long as Larkin considered me a prime suspect he'd have to be skeptical. I had no proof. It was a thing I might have set up myself in an effort to divert suspicion. It could seem almost too pat."

"You were afraid the Inspector might not believe you?"

"Yes."

"Then why should we? . . . Has Dr. Singh identified the poison?"

"He hadn't when I spoke to him around noon. He had eliminated the more common ones, but he said unless he knew what he was looking for, he'd probably have to send a sample off the island."

"And yet you sit here—"

"Because I learned something this afternoon," he said, having no compunction now about the interruption. "When I call him again, and I can do it now if you like, maybe I can tell him what to look for."

Again he had their attention. He was still acutely aware of the girl at his side. When he talked he could not eliminate certain gestures and he had felt his arm brush her shoulder from time to time; he was also still afraid to look at her. Now he seized the moment of silence and hurried on to tell of his visit to Singh's reception room and the books that had been left for him.

He took time to describe their contents and the painstaking search he had made, particularly in the volume on legal medicine. He'd had no preconceived ideas, but had simply considered each category in the hope that he could find anything at all that would provide some starting point.

"And you found one?" Dorothy Atherton's expression remained hostile, her voice openly scornful. "How many listings would you say were in this pharmacology volume?"

"Thousands."

"But you found one that satisfied you? How? . . . Surely you don't expect us to take your word for such an unlikely story?"

This blunt, imperious challenge stirred a thrust of irritation that had been smouldering dormantly for some time and he found a perverse satisfaction now as he gave vent to it.

"You don't have to take my word for one damn thing!" he said roughly. "All we have to do is bring that extension over here." He pointed to the telephone under the awning. "I think if you want to get close when I call Dr. Singh—he was going up the coast with his family but he should be back now—we can hold the earpiece back a bit so we can all hear what he says.

"I'll tell him what I think is in that bottle and ask what the drug I have in mind is used for and in what quantities. What its effects would be in an overdose, what the post-mortem findings are, and who among his patients uses it medicinally . . . Sure," he said, still burning a bit, "it's probably better that way. Then we'll have it on the record for Larkin."

He knew there would be no call. It was all there in the compressed lips, the quick flare of nostrils, the narrowed gaze. People seldom spoke to Dorothy Atherton in that tone and she seemed about to say so. Then her curiosity overcame her resentment.

"Very well," she said coldly. "Suppose *you* tell us about this discovery. Just what was it that enlightened you so?"

"I got the lead from the legal medicine book. Because I didn't know what I was looking for, I started at the beginning. I just kept reading until I found a few paragraphs on a drug that is used medicinally as a tonic in proper dosages and is a deadly poison when used in a certain way; it was also stated that it would go undetected in the ordinary autopsy and could only be discovered in a blood analysis, which is not normally done except perhaps in traffic deaths where a blood-alcohol test might be made."

When he glanced at Dorothy Atherton again he saw that the scorn in her gaze had been replaced by something that he could not identify. Her tone too had changed.

"Then how would the cause of death be listed?"

"As heart failure. It would cause almost immediate ventricular fibrillation, which often happens in an ordinary heart attack. The condition would be irreversible and fatal within a minute or two. If an autopsy showed no brain damage, and nothing significant in the lungs and stomach, the assumption would have to be a heart attack."

"You said, in a certain way. What way?"

"By injection."

"But there was no injection."

"No. And because I'm a layman I can't say for sure if the drug would bring on a fatal heart attack if taken by mouth, or how long it might take. But you see, a layman used it. He knew it was a poison, and it was available, and he took a chance it would do the job."

"And the drug?" Carswell's voice was hushed, and now Maxwell looked at the older man.

"You have a heart problem, don't you, Albert?"

"Not exactly. High blood pressure, yes—"

"Which can lead to a heart attack if not controlled."

"So I'm told."

"And Thursday afternoon when I stopped to see you, you took a pill. Two a day, you said, on doctor's orders. What was the name of that drug?"

"Aldactazide—spelled a-l-d-a-c-t-a-z-i-d-e."

Maxwell looked at Osborne's blunt, weathered face and found it tight and impassive. "That same afternoon when we were on your porch Wanda came out with your medication. You identified it for me. Indocin for the inflammation in your hands, Digitoxin for your heart, aspirin for pain."

"So?"

Maxwell made his explanation to the women.

"When the line about the use of digitalis as a heart tonic gave me a lead, I studied its other qualities. The pharmacology book did the rest. Digitoxin—and I remembered what George had told me—is a trade name used by a certain drug company. There are others with similar qualities, but the base is *digitalis*."

He looked once more at Osborne. "What did you do, George? Use a handful of your Digitoxin? Or was it the old-fashioned tincture of digitalis? The books say it's bitter-tasting, and that little sip I took sure as hell was."

21

THE SILENCE THAT ENVELOPED them and continued for perhaps five seconds was almost palpable. Maxwell, still watching Osborne's face and seeing no change except in a definite
narrowing of the gray eyes, realized his shoulder and neck
were stiff. He straightened, hearing the beginnings of small,
inarticulate sounds, and then Dorothy Atherton, as was her
right and privilege, took command. Turning in her chair,
she called to the maid:

"Grace! . . . Take an order, please. And when you finish,
go into the house and take John with you."

Because he could no longer avoid it, Maxwell turned to
look at Valerie as he waited for his whisky-and-soda. He
saw the troubled lines about the brow at once; but there
was no censure in her eyes, only wonderment and uncertainty and just a faint shadow of fear. He took her hand and
she let him, but it remained limp and unresponsive. Because
it was so important to him, he squeezed to be sure of her
attention.

"You believe me, don't you?"

The wide-open eyes searched his face inch by inch before
she nodded. "George?" she whispered finally. "It—it's just
so hard to believe, to think that—" She tried again. "I know
you wouldn't make a thing like that up, but—"

"George was a very desperate man."

"And you're saying he killed your wife—and that man?"

He had no chance to reply, because when the drinks had been served the hostess was far from satisfied.

"You have made a very serious accusation, Mr. Maxwell. At least, I'm sure we took it as an accusation. Now, assuming that digitalis is found in that bottle of yours, I for one would like to know how and when George put it there?"

"He had plenty of time yesterday morning while I was at Police Headquarters. They came for me early and the club was practically deserted."

He went on to tell how he had questioned the boys who worked at the club. "Only one of them had noticed anyone even near the *Annabel*, and that was a lone fisherman. He couldn't describe him. All he could remember was that the man wore old clothes and a wide-brimmed hat that hid the face; he couldn't say if he was black or white. George would have had workclothes around, and the hat; he could get a dinghy or skiff with no trouble. It wouldn't take two minutes to slip over the side of the *Annabel*, dose the proper bottle, and be back fishing.

"What I don't understand," he said, turning to face Osborne, "is why you had it in for me."

Osborne, who had disdained any previous comment, took a swallow of his pink gin and said:

"It's your story, Maxwell. For myself, I don't know just what the hell you're talking about. I take Digitoxin. I took tincture of digitalis before the doc put me on the new pill. Am I the only one on the island who could have doctored your bottle?"

"You can't buy those things over the counter like aspirin." He turned to Carswell as a new thought came to him. "Yesterday afternoon when you and George came aboard, you said you'd come to check with me; you wanted to know about Blake's plans, and George wondered about my wife's mortgage-note check."

"Yes." Carswell nodded concurrence as he puzzled over the remark. "That's quite true."

"So who suggested your little trip, you or George?"

"Well"—his glance slid to Osborne and he jerked it back —"as a matter of fact, he did."

"I'll bet he did," Maxwell said dryly. "And you know what you would have found when you ducked into the main cabin? Me, Albert. Right where my wife was. And while you were fluttering about trying to find out if I was alive, George would dump the drink I hadn't finished into the sink, tuck the bottle under his jacket, and tell you to stay put while he rowed ashore to phone for a doctor . . . Right, George?" he said, turning to Osborne.

Once again the man remained mute, and this time he had an excuse because Dorothy Atherton demanded her right to the floor. There was determination in every set line of her handsome face, and Maxwell wondered why she was so insistent in preventing any direct questioning of Osborne.

"What rubbish," she said coldly. "That's pure conjecture and you know it. I'll admit your hypothesis is interesting. You even make it sound quite logical. But you still have no proof that George tampered with that bottle—if indeed it was poisoned—on your boat."

"I know it."

"Well, then—"

She made no attempt to finish the sentence. Her glance was haughty and triumphant as she sat back and allowed the inference to be made.

The look did not bother Maxwell. The tension was still building inside him and his nerve ends were acutely sensitive and sharply tuned. He tried to close his mind to thoughts of failure and possible ridicule. For what had been said previously was nothing but worthless prologue unless he could justify it with something more conclusive.

And there might be a way.

The genesis of his idea was a simple observation made

when he had first arrived. This in turn suggested a possible answer to something that had bothered him for some time. His call to Larkin had supplied corroboration for that possibility, and he knew the time had come to make his play and be prepared for the consequences.

He hiked his chair closer to Osborne's. His grin was frozen and humorless but his dark eyes were bright with hope as his glance slid over the man's white-suited figure.

"Stand up a minute, George, will you?"

He saw the startled, uncomprehending stare, the slackened jaw. Because he had half-expected this reaction, he did not let it bother him.

"Come on. Humor me, will you? There's something I'd like to show the others."

Osborne's gray glance flicked away and back. His mouth dipped at the corners and his sneer was both defiant and contemptuous. It was probably pride that made him accept the challenge, but whatever the reason he leaned forward and came to his feet. As he did so Maxwell's eyes focused and his heart flipped and he had trouble keeping control of his facial muscles.

"That's a good-looking suit, George. Lovely material but in some ways impractical, particularly the pants. What I mean is, they're a bit thin, you know?

"I found out with mine that you could see where your undershorts stop. I noticed yours when Valerie and I came up and you limped over to get a drink. I also wondered why one leg of your shorts was longer than the other. If you look down at yourself, you'll see what I mean."

He slid his arm across the back of Osborne's chair as he leaned forward. "And you know what, George? When I began to wonder about that limp, I remembered that you also had a noticeable limp when you came aboard the *Annabel* yesterday morning.

" 'Damned arthritis!' Isn't that what you said? . . . Now we know about your hands, but you used to say you were lucky the condition hadn't spread. So that first limp on the ketch didn't bother me because I wasn't looking for anything. It was different this afternoon."

He paused for breath, and in that uncertain and unwanted moment he was filled with a spasm of distaste for what he was about to do. But he had waited and hoped too long to free himself from the ensnarement this man had thrust upon him.

"You see, something about my wife's murder bothered me, George. The police knew two shots had been fired and one had killed her. When I phoned Larkin, I asked if his men had ever found the other slug in her room. He said no, which made me wonder if that extra-long undershort leg was part of your shorts after all. Maybe it's a bandage—"

The hand on the back of Osborne's chair had been surreptitiously busy while his words demanded attention. Now, with the cane in his right hand, he rapped it smartly across the front of Osborne's left thigh.

The result was instantly explosive, and the man's involuntary yelp was two-toned as he grabbed unthinkingly at his leg. The first part was pure pain with a quick modulation into outraged protest. When he straightened with a conscious and exaggerated movement, his rugged face was gray, the eyes filled with misery and despair.

Maxwell carefully replaced the cane, feeling an odd muscular and nervous weakness take over now and hearing the startled exclamations about him.

"I think that's where the missing slug is. Right, George?" he said quietly. "And I think Inspector Larkin will find some legal means to have a look. If that slug—and it must still be there—matches the one Dr. Singh removed from my wife—"

He let the sentence hang and watched with wide-eyed surprise as Dorothy Atherton stood up and marched straight-backed past the awning and through the French doors.

22

IN THE THIRTY SECONDS it took Dorothy Atherton to return, no one said a word. The aftereffects of shock still lingered, immobilizing and silencing all of them. Maxwell stared unseeing at the distant sea, only now realizing how the tension had been building inside him. The sudden impact of his success and the knowledge that his long-shot hunch had paid off, made him keenly aware of some new muscular weakness; with it came a sense of relief that filmed his body with sweat. What snapped him out of it was a sharp and startled cry from Valerie.

"*Mother!*"

He saw the reason for the exclamation when he brought his head up. For, as the woman marched back to her chair, he stared in open amazement at the double-barreled shotgun she carried in the crook of one elbow. Looking neither right nor left, she sat down and placed the gun squarely across her lap, the muzzle pointing toward the swimming pool.

Her very presence commanded a new silence. Maxwell had started at the astonishing sight of the tall, dignified, unshakable figure and her shotgun. He knew instinctively that she was totally sincere, but all he felt then was the welcome realization that it was over for him.

The gun intimidated no one, since none of them had any intention of provoking her. Yet somehow the gesture, absurd as it was, seemed completely in character . . .

He had been aware of Valerie's first horrified reaction, and now he listened and silently applauded her efforts as she tried to treat this new and unexpected development with a studied casualness that was at once forced and brittle. "What's that for?" she demanded. "Do you expect, as the American Westerns put it, to shoot up the joint?"

"I hope it won't be necessary to shoot anything," the woman said woodenly, ignoring her daughter's attempt at humor. "But I intend to see that George has whatever time he needs to think things over and leave with dignity."

"And you're afraid Albert or Alan might try to stop him?"

"I was thinking more of the Inspector. If he should happen to arrive before we're ready for him he might feel dutybound to make an arrest. I have six's here, I believe." She patted the gun. "A few in the ankle or foot should discourage him . . . Because you see, it's my fault, really. It was my idea from the very beginning."

"Your idea to what?"

"After that disgusting scene here Friday afternoon I was fully determined to kill that woman before I'd let her ruin Michael's life and Wanda's."

She looked at Maxwell as though she had never seen him before. "If I could reach such a conclusion in the three or four times I saw her, I can't understand how you could have avoided murder while you were living with her."

She expected no reply but Maxwell gave her one. "I've often wondered myself, Mrs. Atherton. The idea came to me more than once." He eyed her thoughtfully, trying to analyze her mood and attitude before he continued. "You said it was your idea. How did you intend to pull it off?"

"In the simplest way possible. We talked it over, George and I, because we both wanted the same thing. I knew the Villa Inn when it was a private estate. I knew how to get to that bungalow without using the drive. I told George that sometime in the middle of the night I'd simply go there and do what had to be done."

"But Mother—" Valerie had leaned forward, clasped hands between her thighs. Traces of shock and disbelief still clouded her eyes; she could not accept all she had heard. "How did you hope to get in? How did—"

"I hoped the door might be unlocked." Dorothy Atherton said in the same blunt convincing way, "and if not, I should have knocked until she opened it. I'm twice as big as she was and twice as strong. I should have grabbed her and put one hand over her mouth and carried her to the bed and put a pillow over her face and held it there until I was sure she was dead.

"Furthermore, I'm quite sure I could have managed without being seen. In fact, I was hopeful that I would never be accused. Even if I was, how could I be convicted? A woman, a nasty woman, dies of suffocation. Any investigation would get nowhere; it would finally be dropped.

"It was all very simple and clear-cut, the way I saw it. But George"—she shook her head sadly as she looked over at him—"argued that it was his job, not mine. He pointed out that he could have a fatal heart attack any day, that he had little to lose, and that he had to be sure Wanda would be Mrs. Michael Atherton and someday be mistress of the Hall.

"He insisted that he try first. He would go to her place when she was alone. He would threaten her, swear he would kill her if she did not leave the island. If that didn't work, he could do what had to be done with his bare hands and take his chances. Oh, we were prepared to pay if we had to, I think. But it didn't have to happen that way. If she hadn't snatched up that gun when George—"

"She must have had it under the pillow," Osborne said, awe and distance in the cadence of his voice. "I hadn't touched her; I didn't intend to, not then. It was in her hand before I knew it and I saw that crazy mean look in her eyes. When she turned it on me—I wasn't three feet away—I had to go for it. I felt the bullet slap my leg. I knew there'd be another. I grabbed it and twisted and it went off again.

"I didn't realize I'd taken the gun until I was halfway back to our table. Luckily I wasn't bleeding much and I had dark slacks on and it didn't show. You were back a couple of minutes after I was, and we were standing and I was holding the napkin in front of me."

Maxwell nodded, remembering, willing to believe that what he had just heard was the truth.

"I'd managed to tell Dorothy why we had to leave in a hurry," Osborne said in the same dull tones. "She suggested Wanda stay with you but when Wanda asked us to drop her off at home it made things even easier for me."

"I brought George up here," Dorothy said. "I had treated enough cuts and slashes on field hands to know what to do. I cleaned the wound—it was only a tiny puckered hole—and sprinkled some sulpha in it and put a bandage on."

"It didn't bother me much then," Osborne said. "And then later I went back and moved—"

"Why, George?" Maxwell said. "Just what did you hope to prove? You didn't expect the police to think she'd been killed there, did you? Why pick on me?"

"Because I was afraid you had seen me. I wanted to make sure you were suspected."

"Seen you?" Maxwell squinted, his dark stare puzzled and incredulous. "When?"

"Just after I'd left the bungalow. You were coming down the path and looking right at me before I could duck into the bushes."

He paused, awaiting some reaction, and now Maxwell's mind flashed back and it was there, like a film clip sliding too quickly through a viewer. He *had* thought someone was there; he had nearly called out . . . He shook his head.

"All I saw was a shadowy figure that moved, George. I wasn't even sure of that."

Osborne sighed and his shoulders slumped. "I didn't know. I was afraid to let it pass. I couldn't go to the police and say I'd seen you approaching the bungalow—that would involve me. An unsupported anonymous call would have been worthless. I suppose all I wanted was to involve you and confuse the police."

"George!" Dorothy Atherton's voice was reproachful and demanded attention. "Is it true, about the poison? You didn't tell me about that."

"I was too ashamed. I knew it was a mistake after I'd come back home. I have no excuse. Panic, desperation—I don't know. The leg was stiffening. I couldn't have the bullet removed here, but I knew a doctor in Port of Spain. With Maxwell dead and still under suspicion and the police trying to make a case, I thought they'd let me leave, at least for overnight."

He took another breath and looked at Maxwell, his eyes anguished, as though asking somehow for understanding.

"I can't expect you to believe me now, Alan, but I was never more relieved at anything in my life than I was when I saw your head pop out of the main hatch when we hailed you yesterday morning. I never had anything against you. I suppose I was just too mixed up and frightened to know what I was doing. And then Leon Carr came along and made things worse."

Carswell, who had remained mute and motionless, apparently could deny his thirst no longer. He rose and moved unobtrusively to the drink table. When he came back, his bony hand was trembling, and he brought up the other hand to steady the glass while he drank.

"If I had picked the one time when my little project had no chance whatever of success, that was it," Osborne said as he watched Carswell sit down. "I not only thought you had seen me, I found out later that Carr had also been a witness . . . He said he'd been out for a cigarette on the edge of the parking area," he added. "When he saw me start down the path he did the only logical thing a man like him could do—"

"He followed you," Maxwell prompted.

"He moved round to that high window to listen in. He heard the two shots, heard the door close when I left. He also spotted you coming down the path, so he stayed right where he was. As soon as you had left he sneaked inside.

"He told me later he'd had an argument with your wife about his fee and he knew that with her dead he wouldn't get paid. After he'd taken those two pieces of jewelry he had but one thought in his mind: to get off the island with them. To go to the police with his information was something that would never occur to him, so he made me an offer."

Maxwell, wanting to get all of it, asked, "When was this?"

"Saturday, just before noon. He said he'd give me the traveler's checks, which he said I'd have no trouble cashing, and a chance to run. I was supposed to steal a boat—he even suggested I take yours, which would have been possible—and work my way through the islands. He would phone the police an anonymous tip, and with me gone and apparently running from arrest the heat, as he put it, would be off and he'd have a chance to leave the island with his precious jewelry.

"I told him I had to think it over but I knew then I had no choice because I had to believe him when he said if I wasn't off the island before morning—that is, today—he'd turn me in.

"That's why I was waiting on the roof with the gun I'd kept when you entered his room," he said.

"You got there ten minutes too late," Maxwell said.

"I didn't dare go there until it was dark. But I knew in the instant I fired that it was you and not Carr. It was no more than a glimpse, a sort of profile view, but it was sufficient. When the light went out, I also knew, and believe me I was glad, that I had missed."

He took another visible breath and looked at nothing with vacant eyes.

"As soon as I could, I telephoned the Villa Inn because I knew somehow that Carr would be there. He was. I told him I was ready to run and I wanted those traveler's checks. I told him where to meet me. I was waiting. When he stopped the car I walked over, leaned in the window, fired twice, and threw the gun in beside him. I then went home and got very drunk."

He stopped abruptly, his exhaustion obvious to all. After a moment Dorothy Atherton shifted the shotgun, and when she spoke there was a curious gentleness in her voice Maxwell had never heard before.

"There is still a little time, George. You can find some sort of boat. No one knows the Grenadines like you do."

Osborne shook his head and a smile touched his weathered, graying face. "And make you an accessory, Dorothy? I don't think so. Even if I got away for a while, the odds would catch up with me. I'm surprised you don't see the morbid irony in the situation."

He grunted softly, an ambiguous sound. "I suppose it comes back to the drug I used, fortunately without success, on Alan. These Digitoxin pills are somewhat recent with me. I had some tincture of digitalis left, and that's what I poured into the brandy bottle. I have enough pills for several days, but once I run out I can only wait for the final attack.

"And since there is no other way, why not use what I have at home and get it over with? It amounts to the same thing in the end, and why should we give the press a field day? There will most certainly be some reporters here by tomorrow. Let's hope it will be nothing more than someone from the Barbados and Port of Spain dailies. By then Larkin—naturally I'll leave a note for him—will have the story neatly packaged for them. A word from you to the Governor and Attorney General should keep the publicity to a minimum, at least here. Wanda will be all right once she understands. She's a sensible girl and stronger than you might think."

He said other things, but Maxwell was no longer listening as he became aware of some acute inner sickness brought on by the knowledge that Osborne was caught without hope of escape. He also understood that if he, Maxwell, had been motivated by any small thoughts of vengeance in his determination to clear himself, such thoughts had long since been discarded.

He watched Osborne stand up and reach for his cane and it occurred to him with startling clarity that any thoughts of pity would be misplaced. For death by hanging was still on the books in St. Vincent, and Osborne had been granted a much easier way.

That thought remained until Osborne's mood took an unexpected turn. He was gazing reflectively at the distant sea when he laughed shortly, a harsh sound but surprisingly free from bitterness. He looked at Dorothy Atherton.

"It didn't quite work out the way we thought it might, but perhaps the end result will be the same for Wanda and Michael."

The woman already had him by the arm, and as they moved away Maxwell heard her say, "It will, George. I promise. She'll need him more than ever now and before the year is out she'll be living right here at the Hall."

She walked with him to the corner of the house, the shotgun in one hand. She put the other arm around Osborne as they stopped long enough for a final embrace; then he was gone and she came back, her eyes full and her cheeks wet. But her head was still high and she looked neither right nor left and it was Valerie who, having come to her feet, provided a welcome digression.

"Mother." She waited until the woman stopped; then pointed at the shotgun. "You wouldn't really have used it, would you?"

Dorothy Atherton regarded her daughter, a quick affection showing through the tears.

"Only as a threat. It *was* a rather melodramatic gesture, wasn't it? Particularly since it wasn't loaded . . . *Grace!*"

The little maid, who must have been stationed just inside the French doors, appeared as if by magic. When the woman handed her the gun and told her to put it back she marched off, holding it in both hands as if bearing a salver.

By that time Maxwell had Valerie by the hand. She still was not ready to look at him but she let herself be led to the table under the awning. He said they both needed drinks and made them. When he turned she was standing close and now she leaned forward an inch or two, head still bowed as she put her face in the angle between his neck and shoulder.

They stood that way a second or two, not moving until Maxwell put the drinks aside. When he put his hands on her waist she came to him and he felt the slight tremor in the firm curve of her back before she relaxed.

An unexpected shout from the corner of the house broke the spell, and when Maxwell stepped back he saw that the boy in the white jacket who had been tending bar had apparently been stationed in front of the house for a purpose.

"The Inspector's car come, ma'am! Just now turn in the drive."

They took their drinks with them, and Dorothy Atherton, who had been saying something to Carswell, looked right at Maxwell.

"I suppose I should thank you for coming here with your

story and suspicions instead of going directly to Inspector
Larkin, and I hope I may make a small request. I had better
go wash my face now, and I would appreciate it if you
would entertain the Inspector." The faintest of smiles flick-
ered in the blue eyes and was gone. "If you try hard, you
should be able to occupy him with your story for at least
as long as you entertained us, don't you think?"

She left then and Carswell went back for a refill. Maxwell saw that the girl was all right now, and her eyes were
soft and approving over the rim of the glass as she sipped
her gin-and-tonic.

"I suppose this"—she waved emptily toward the front of
the house—"will take quite a while."

Maxwell said probably. "And in case we don't have a
chance to get together again . . ."

She cut him off right there. "Oh, but we will. When the
Inspector finishes with us down at Police Headquarters,
you'll have to bring me home, won't you?"

This simple forthright invitation pleased him immeasur-
ably. He wanted to grab her again and squeeze hard, but
he settled for a wide grin.

"All right, but I'd like to get one thing clear. I won't be
able to see you off tomorrow afternoon but I'll be at the
airstrip when you come back. Until then, please remember
what I said about that hotel guy in Barbados."

This time the smile was mischievous. "You mean I
shouldn't take him too seriously?"

Maxwell said that was exactly what he meant, and something about her expression that he did not try to analyze
told him all he wanted to know.

A Note About the Author

George Harmon Coxe was born in Olean, New York, and spent his youth there and in nearby Elmira. After a year at Purdue and one at Cornell, he worked for five years with newspapers in California, Florida, and New York, and did advertising for a New England printer for five more. Since that time he has devoted himself to writing—for two years with Metro-Goldwyn-Mayer, then as a free lance, selling numerous short stories, novelettes, and serials to magazines as well as to motion-picture, radio, and television producers.

He is a past president of the Mystery Writers of America, and winner of its Grand Master Award in 1964.

A NOTE ON THE TYPE

The text of this book is set in Caledonia, a Linotype face that belongs to the family of printing types called "modern face" by printers—a term used to mark the change in style of type-letters that occurred about 1800. Caledonia borders on the general design of Scotch Modern, but is more freely drawn than that letter.

This book was composed, printed
and bound by The Haddon Craftsmen,
Inc., Scranton, Pa.

Typography by Virginia Tan.
Binding design by Guy Fleming.